Black Boy Lost, Black Girl Adrift

Will you find us?

Ryan Hodge

SMP PUBLISHING

SMP Publishing Edition

Printed in the United States of America

10 9 8 7 6 5 4 3 2 1

ISBN: 978-0-9977990-3-3 (PBK)

DEDICATION

Dear Ma,

You always covered us with a blanket of love and
security,
It was crystal clear love and loyalty, never doubt,
never obscurity.
I'm often reminded that you're still here when I hear
phrases you'd say,
Or when you visit me in my dreams and we discuss
topics from present day.
It seems like you never left and that you exist in a
different way,
I always look forward to seeing you my dreams or in a
symbol each day.
Your presence, while living physically was a present
beyond worldly value,
From day one, you were our Mom, provider, advice
giver, and a pal too.
I'm thankful to have known you and been able to
have the fortified bond that we did,
Our relationship only got stronger from the days
when I was a kid.
It's safe to say that you're an angel with wings,
I look forward to your next visit and the joy it brings.
We love you for your strengths and weaknesses; we
love you all ways,
Our love for you is never-ending; we love you always.

CHAPTER 1
Christopher's Perspective

My name is Chris and I'm a senior at Shabazz High School in Newark, New Jersey. I'll just go ahead and admit that I'm fucked up! I'm not fucked up in the sense that I got into a fight and lost or that I'm intoxicated, but I'm fucked up in the sense that life is difficult and making the right decisions on a day to day or even moment to moment basis is a cumbersome task. Every day is a constant struggle against other people and within myself. I can't get right. Being a black teenager in a bad neighborhood makes for very turbulent living conditions. These streets are tough and will eat you alive if you're not tougher. If you show any sign of weakness, the wolves will swoop in on you. At that point, you'll only have two choices. You either allow them to eat you alive or become one of them and help them eat others alive. Which one would you do? Either option you choose puts you in a fucked up spot.

Today is the first day of school of my senior year. My sister and I are headed to school to see what this first day has in store for us. My sister, Kennedy is my heart and soul. We're extremely close and inseparable for the most part. I guess it's only right that we're so close because we're twins. I was born thirteen minutes before her, so that makes me the oldest and it's my job to protect her. We agree on most things and rarely have any conflict between us. She always has my back and I always have hers. We live in a rundown apartment building on Milford Avenue, so the walk to school is very short, but is never uneventful.

My sister and I are walking to school when we see a fairly disheveled individual walking towards us. We know that he's a fiend because we've seen him around plenty of times. Even though we've seen him on many occasions, we never get comfortable around him. We've seen too many fiends spaz out at the drop of a dime to let our guards down. His actions are totally unpredictable and can't be calculated when he really needs a hit. Kennedy and I decide to cross the street just to be safe. Unfortunately, the man crosses the street as we do.

Kennedy speaks, "Like bruh, here we go with the bullshit! I know he's gonna say some dumb shit. It's always something."

"I know sis. Damn, we can't even walk a couple of blocks without some fucked up shit happening. Listen, if he tries anything, I'm gonna fuck him up and you bounce. I don't want anything to happen to you," I say.

"Hell no! Bruh, if he tries you, we're jumping him. I'm not leaving while you fight him. You crazy as hell," Kennedy replies.

We continue walking up the street as the fiend approaches us. My sister clutches her bag firmly just in case he tries to snatch and run. I clinch my fists tightly just in case I have to throw the hands with this man. He's walking awkwardly as the distance between us shortens. He vacillates between rubbing his nose and neck. The unkempt man is very fidgety and I can tell that he needs a hit. He stops walking and stands in the middle of the sidewalk.

"You straight?" he asks.

"No, I'm not straight," I answer in an aggravated tone.

The man doesn't take my response to be true, so he asks again and I give him the same response. My sister and I continue walking and the guy follows us. This man is clearly sick because he grabs my sister's shoulder to get her attention. She pulls her shoulder away from the man. Simultaneously, I swing at the man and punch him in the face. He stumbles a few feet, but doesn't fall. I grab my sister and put her behind me and take a defensive stance.

"I don't want any trouble. I just was gonna ask her if she was holding," the man states.

"Son, I told you that it wasn't nothing happening. You shoulda kept stepping. Don't you ever touch my fucking sister," I yell with bits of spit flying from my mouth.

I want to pummel the guy, but Kennedy's holding me back. She knows it's not worth it to beat him down. I'm irate, but the guy doesn't pose an immediate threat, so I walk off with my sister. This type of stuff is the reason why I'm always on edge. I have serious trust issues and feel like everyone's out to get me and my sister. Really, she's the only person I trust with everything. My temper is awful when it comes to my sister. I'm fairly rational for the most part, but I tend to lose it when my sister is distressed.

"Damn, we can't even walk to school without some shit popping off! What the fuck!" I complain to Kennedy as we walk.

"Shit, I know right. He's lucky I didn't cut his ass. I was like 2.5 from pulling out my razor and slicing him. I was about to be on some fuck it type shit," Kennedy words.

I voice, "That's what I'm saying. Then we probably woulda got in trouble because he was on some other shit."

This situation is one reason why I'm so fucked up out here. I have to walk to school with the threat of violence highly possible every day. That in itself is a deterrent to even go to school. I never know if a walk to school will be my or Kennedy's last walk. How can I really focus on school today after what just happened? For all I know, that same man could be waiting for me after school. What's stopping him from coming back at the end of the school day and hitting me over the head with a brick? I'm tasked with getting good grades while trying to survive the dangers of the streets. I bet if we were white kids in the suburbs, we wouldn't have to endure this nonsense. Why does my life matter less than another person's does?

I know I'm going to be on edge all day. We make it to school and stand outside waiting for the bell to ring. My sister and I talk to some classmates who we haven't seen since school let out for summer break. A lot of people have on new gear, but Kennedy and I don't. Everyone's standing around comparing who has on what and who's the best dressed. Going crazy over this material stuff is really pointless. We're not buying into it.

The bell is going to ring in two more minutes. I'm really not ready to start the school day, but it is what it is. I normally wouldn't mind standing out here waiting for the bell because it's pretty warm out this morning; however, some kids with new clothes on are roasting other kids who have on beat down gear. I don't like seeing people who are less fortunate than others being picked on because of their circumstance. It's just not right to me. It's almost like somebody white judging you because you're black. Either way, being poor or black is out of our hands, so we shouldn't be antagonized because of it. Another reason I don't want to be near people being bullied, is because I know where it normally ends.

Kennedy orates, "Bruh, I hope the bell rings soon because you already know what's gonna happen if it doesn't. I ain't got time for no more drama."

"I was just thinking the same damn thing. I can tell that the girl over there in the black leggings is getting heated. She gonna hook off, watch!" I verbalize.

"I know. I don't even be on it like that, but I ain't gonna let anybody try me. Fuck that! We'll just have to throw the hands," voices Kennedy frankly.

"Word. Yo, the bell is taking forever! You know I know how you do," I say.

Finally, the bell rings. We all start walking towards the entrance to the school. There are so many students out here trying to get into the building at this one entrance that it starts to bottleneck. We're standing still waiting to enter when it happens. The girl who was getting cracked on by the other girl starts hollering at the top of her lungs. She's clearly irate. The two girls are now standing face to face.

"Bitch, I'm tired of you running your damn mouth! For real," she says.

The girl responds, "You ain't gonna do shit though, so shut the fuck up. You're a broke ass basic bitch."

The students can clearly tell that a fight is about to go down. The entire crowd watching starts screaming "World Star"! Students are running back and forth as if they've been given a shot of adrenaline. My sister and I freeze in our tracks because we don't care about this drama one bit. We don't want to try to squeeze past because they may start to fight as we're doing so. We decide to stand back and let whatever is going to happen play out.

Both of their faces are donning looks of disgust for the other person. Many students are promoting the fight. I'm just hoping that some of the school administrators come before they start throwing blows. Quite a few students in the crowd are blocking the doorway to get into the school and have taken their phones out. A lot of them are on Facebook Live, so they can broadcast everything to the world in real time.

The girls have had enough trash talking and eventually throw up their hands to engage in physical combat. My sister and I just look from a distance and shake our heads because it's always something going on. Everyday has a new set of predicaments and unfortunate events. We move further away from the crowd because we know that once the fight starts, the crowd could shift in any direction without notice. We've seen other fights start just because someone bumped into someone else during a fight.

One of the girls throws a series of punches and connects to the other girl's face. The girl who was doing the bullying really should have kept her mouth shut because she's the one who's getting punched in the face. She's stumbling back as she's getting hit and loses her footing. To her detriment, she falls to the ground. The other girl jumps on top of her and continues punching her in the face. Next, she commences to bang the girl's head into the ground. This fight is totally one sided and needs to be stopped. Unfortunately, no one is making a move to stop it. Finally, the girl stops pummeling her and stands up as she taunts her verbally. The girl on the ground is clearly incapacitated, but that doesn't stop the beating. Next, the girl kicks her in the face.

"Bitch, you fucked with the wrong one today! You got your ass beat for nothing. I told you that I ain't nothing to play with," she boasts arrogantly.

The entire crowd is cheering as if they're watching a sporting event. You'd think this was a joyous event by the way people are behaving. My sister and I are disgusted by all of this. It's the first day of school and all of this is happening. We're even more shocked that the school administration hasn't even made it over here yet. Finally, the crowd starts to dissipate and we're able to head inside the school. The video of the fight is being shared hundreds of times on social media. Kennedy and I make it to homeroom just before the late bell rings. What a terrible start to the school day.

CHAPTER 2
Kennedy's Perspective

My brother and I make it to third period with no more drama. The first two periods were boring because we didn't get to do anything other than listen to the teachers' rules. The teachers gave out the course syllabi like they normally do. I'm so over high school. I'm ready for college or whatever my next life endeavor will be. I just know growing up and living in the hood is for the birds. My brother and I talk everyday about how tough things are here for us. It's a constant battle of right versus wrong. Additionally, the line between what's right and wrong seems to be obscured. Somehow, we still remain positive through it all.

Class starts and the teacher begins to take attendance. She actually made it through the entire roster without messing up a single person's name. I think this has to be a first in all my years of schooling. I whisper to my brother the hilarity of the teacher not messing up anyone's name and my brother shares my same humor for this anomaly. The teacher goes over her rules and regulations like the other teachers have, but she's not boring like them. Mrs. Smith is her name and she has style. Her outfit is very well coordinated and her delivery is very smooth. Surprisingly, she even has a few funny jokes.

Mrs. Smith informs us that she's a first-year teacher who just graduated from Howard University in D.C. I can tell she's fresh out of college because she's mad young. Hopefully, she'll be a good fit for our class. Normally, young teachers are very fun to have. The more she talks, the more I begin to like her. A bunch of the guys in class including my brother are checking her out. Her swag is on ten right now. Mrs. Smith is definitely lit!

I really need to use the restroom. I raise my hand and ask permission to leave class. Mrs. Smith grants me permission to go. I walk to the restroom and head to the middle stall. While I'm in the stall, I hear someone enter the bathroom and go into the stall beside me. I don't think anything of it until I hear a boy's voice. At first, I just figure that the girl who came in was on the phone even though the boy's voice didn't seem like it was coming through a phone. Being suspicious, I look down to the floor and see a boy's pair of boots along with a female's pair of shoes. Wow!!!

The girl and guy are in the stall together. I know it's about to go down in there. I need to get out of here as quickly as possible. The only thing that they can possibly be about to do is fuck and I don't want to hear it. That's just nasty. Why do they have to handle their business in here while I'm in here? I know they could have found somewhere off campus to go.

"Put him in your mouth," the boy says.

I hear what sounds like a zipper being zipped down and a belt buckle being unfastened. Next, I hear the sound of a dick being sucked on. The boy is moaning while she gives him head. This is crazy as hell to say the least. Finally, I finish tinkling and flush the toilet. I exit the stall and walk over to the sink. I thought that flushing the toilet would have made them stop, but it didn't. Shockingly, it made them even more passionate about what they're doing. I can hear the girl sucking harder and the guy moaning even louder. I wash my hands and beeline for the door. To my surprise, there are two more boys posted up by the water fountain by the bathroom door. They're not fooling me. I know they're waiting to go in the bathroom and get served by the girl in the stall giving head. I'm just glad they didn't all go in there while I was in there. I would've lost my mind.

I feel sorry for that girl. It's just real messed

up that she felt she had to do that in the stall. I make it back to class just in time for an ice breaker activity. I link up with my brother and some random dude who neither one of us knows. While we work on the assignment, I tell my brother about the girl and guy in the bathroom. My brother just shakes his head and tells me about times he's seen the same thing happen in the boy's bathrooms and even in the stairwells.

We finish and present the ice breaker activities to the class. The presentations are extremely fun and make the class time go by fast. I'm going to like Mrs. Smith's class; I can tell already. We pack up our belongings and wait for the bell to ring. By the time we get in the hallway, students are going crazy over a "bop" video that's being shared on The Gram. Someone made a video of the girl giving head in the bathroom stall from earlier. I'm not surprised because that entire scenario was beyond reckless.

We're standing in the hallway when several dudes are surrounding the girl who they're saying was the one sucking dick in the bathroom. Several dudes are asking her to give them blowjobs too. She's telling them that it wasn't her and that she doesn't do that, but they don't believe her. Unfortunately, it's her in the video and everyone knows it. Apparently, my brother and I are standing next to two of the guys whose dicks she sucked.

"That bitch got some good ass head, son! I

bussed in her mouth early," one guy says arrogantly.

"Hell yeah! I had dat bitch choking on my shit too. I ain't gonna front though, I came fast as hell. I just started fucking her face from the door. I ain't even talk to her. I just whipped my shit out and shoved it in her mouth," another guy narrates.

They shoot more vulgar comments back and forth betwixt one another. They're referring to that girl as if she's an animal or something less than a person. Moments later, the girl in the video approaches the two guys talking about her. She has a very troubled and concerned look on her face. I would be concerned too if someone had a video of me performing oral sex on several people in a bathroom stall. Fortunately, for me, that's never going to happen because I'm never going to do it.

Sex is a special and private act between two people who care for one another. I get that it's also fun, but that doesn't mean that it's supposed to be treated like a daily activity with no meaning behind it. I don't see how these girls let multiple dudes fuck them like their bodies aren't temples to be respected and cherished. I'm not interested in having sex with the entire student body; that's just not my thing. Also, my brother would hang me if I did things like that. Chris plays no games when it comes to me and stuff like that. I'm glad I have him watching my back.

She asks, "Why did you two share that video? You know that was some fuck shit, right?"

"Yo, chill with that bullshit! I didn't share shit, so don't come for me like that. My battery been dead since the end of first period," one dude responds.

The next guy chimes in, "I took the video, but I didn't share it. Somebody must have used my phone and shared the video. I didn't find out until after the fact, so don't blame me. Shit, it ain't my fault either."

She voices, "That's real fucked up that y'all did me like that. That was supposed to be between us. I thought we was supposed to be cool. Y'all shitted on me for real for real. Now, everybody roasting me for what we did."

"Really though? We didn't do shit! You was the one sucking dick. All we did was get our shit sucked," one student replies.

The other guy verbalizes, "Listen, I'm heading to class. This conversation is pointless. Ain't nobody force you to give us head and you knew we were recording, so miss me with the dumb shit cuz you know we weren't cool like that. I don't know you like that. You like a thot now, so don't even speak to me in the hallway when you see me. I'm out."

One of the dudes walks away and leaves the other guy and the girl standing there. They talk for another minute or so. The guy remaining there pretty much tells her the same thing. He explains to her that he can't be involved with her on a serious note because she's on tape giving multiple dudes head. She tells him that they're the ones who recorded the act and pressured her to give them head to begin with. Apparently, he's had enough because he walks off and leaves her standing by herself.

I don't know the girl at all, but she's broken and hurt. Even if I did know her, I wouldn't know what to tell her to help her feel any better. I'm sure she's feeling a bit trashy right now and I don't blame her. Clearly, she didn't envision the shit storm that she's in right now. She probably thought it was going to be all good and nobody would find out. Unfortunately, that is totally not the case. In another hour, the entire student body will have seen or at least heard about the presence of the "bop" video.

I feel sorry for her and the situation that she's cast herself into. Her poor judgment has landed her into the conundrum that she's presently in. Unfortunately, she's not too different from many other females her age or even older. Societal norms are working against her too. I can't deny that anyone could be in her shoes in a blink of an eye.

The reason I say societal norms are working against her is because sex is something that we are constantly bombarded with. The pressures to have sex and to be sexy are in everything that we do. For example, sex is regularly being introduced to us through music, social media, fashion, and movies. The regular availability of sex in our lives desensitizes us to it and makes it a way of life. I hear females younger than me talking about things they've done sexually because they were influenced by music. One girl let two dudes run a train on her because a song suggested it. That's how powerful music is in the lives of teenagers.

How can a girl resist the constant pressure from many facets in her life to have sex? We are in a damned if we do and damned if we don't type of situation. What do I mean? What I mean is that women are in a situation where if they engage in sex with people they're damned and if they don't they're damned. It's a no win situation for us. I'll use the girl in the bathroom giving oral sex to prove my point.

Many boys pressure females everyday about having sex with them. I'm sure they pressure us to have sex with them because they're pressured by their peers to have sex. Guys meet females and try everything possible to get into their panties. This puts females in a very precarious situation. The girl has a very important decision to make at this juncture in life. She has to decide to have sex with the guy or not to have sex with him. There's a lot riding on her decision. It's not just as simple as deciding yes or no. It's a decision that's filled with consequence and that's why women grapple with this choice so much.

The girl whose being pressured to have sex may genuinely like the person who's asking, so that already lends itself to her giving in to the sexual advances. She has to consider what will happen if she doesn't give in to the pursuit. Will the person making the advances stop dealing with her and go to someone who's willing to have sex? Chances are that's what's going to happen, so she misses out. Another possibility is that the word will get around that a girl is not fucking, so now guys won't ask her to go on dates because they aren't going to get any. Guys aren't willing to waste their time pursuing one girl for sex if they can get it across the street. Sadly, the female who's saving herself will not be as popular as the girl who is "giving it up" and will spend many nights alone.

To relate my point to the girl in the bathroom stall, she decided to give in to the advances of the guys who wanted sex. As we've seen, that didn't work out so well for her. The guys, before she gave them what they wanted, were willing to talk to her and send her messages. She was under the impression that she was cool with those guys, but they really weren't cool with her. She was just a means for the dudes to get another notch on their belts. Nothing more and nothing less.

The guys communicated with her and once they got what they wanted, they left her high and dry. Those boys don't want anything to do with her and have already moved on to their next victim. I know they didn't force themselves on her, but society forced her into that situation. That poor girl was exploited by society and she doesn't even know it. The entire student body knows what she has done, so now she's labeled a thot. No one's going to take her seriously from this point forward. She's now going to be spending a lot of nights by herself.

One girl who doesn't have sex isn't being asked out because she has a reputation for not giving up the goods. Another girl gives up the goods, so she can be asked out and taken on dates and is eventually ostracized for the very thing that got her asked out to begin with. Ultimately, both girls are spending a lot of time alone trying to figure out what they should do to be accepted. It's crazy how two females can make totally different decisions and still find themselves in the same situation. They're damned if they do and damned if they don't.

REFLECTION

We all know that this is a problem that exists throughout this country if not, the world. This problem of our nation being over-sexualized has to be tackled head on if it's going to be reduced or ended altogether. Often times, society talks about problems, but doesn't offer answers or solutions to them. Today's youth need to be approached and counseled starting at an early age.

The question becomes what can they be counseled on that will be effective in ending this over-sexualized nation. The age-old answer is that educating the youth starts at home. That's the easiest answer in the world, but it seems to be a cop out answer. That answer almost takes the blame off of society as a whole and places responsibility solely on parents. Don't get me wrong, family members should be responsible for raising and educating their children, but that doesn't remove society from the equation.

Government has many roles when it comes to what it's supposed to provide for its citizens. One duty in particular is to promote the welfare of its body of people. I mention this for a very specific reason. Let's say the job of the family is to raise and provide for its youth. I totally agree with that statement. The dilemma our youth face today is that they aren't being properly cared for by family members. If nobody steps in to help or save them, there will be millions of children being raised by the streets, by people who are ill-prepared for the task at hand, and they'll raise themselves, or they'll be raised by the media.

Since we know family structures are breaking down, making statements that educating our youth starts at the home is really a moot point. It's not happening at the home, so it has to happen elsewhere. Children can't go without being exposed to information just because it's not being provided at home. If a child wasn't being fed at home, the government would step in and feed the child and this is no different because it all ties into the overall health of the child. The question becomes what entity takes the responsibility for the welfare of the youth. The answer is the school system. The school system is tasked with educating the country's youth, so it's only right that they pick up the slack.

Students in school take a myriad of classes each day. Depending on the type of schedule the school follows, students may have the same classes every day or every other day. Also, the number of classes they attend each day vary according to the system the school follows. Students take a myriad of math, English, and science classes just to name a few. Many students contend that all of the classes they take aren't highly beneficial. In fact, they further contend that some classes are totally useless. I've taught hundreds of students who reported that the school system as it stands today, doesn't meet most of their needs.

Unfortunately, the school system hasn't changed at the rate that the world has changed. The school system isn't teaching real world scenarios and situations that many of today's youth face. I graduated high school almost twenty years ago and the schools are still teaching Romeo and Juliet as well as The Crucible. The students simply don't relate to the text and may not benefit from it. So what should the schools do?

The school system needs courses that all girls and boys take regularly that focus on real world issues. To address the issue of hyper-sexualized youth, there should be a curriculum that promotes self-esteem and confidence. The course would discuss other things that give people value besides sex. It should discuss what sound decision making is. Being your own person can be taught and that not conforming to the group is okay. The definition of what a man and a woman is should also be included in the class. Children are constantly bombarded with the promotion of sex, so it's only right that they're exposed to things that help them combat that constant message. If not, students will continue to be overtaken by this sex craze.

This course would provide the conversations and teachings that many of our youth aren't getting at home. Currently, our youth find themselves in chaotic situations and don't have the slightest idea of how to navigate them, so they make a decision in that moment and in many cases, it's the wrong decision. They may go along with the group just to fit in or because their fragile self-esteem has been challenged. If you teach a person how to handle adverse or unpopular situations, you have a better chance of them performing adequately. Contrarily, if you teach them nothing, they have nothing to refer to, so they'll most likely find themselves in a quagmire. In life, many people will sway, but if they're taught properly, they will always make it back to their moral compass. If the school's mission is to prepare students for the challenges of the twenty-first century, they need to teach things that will help their students get there.

CHAPTER 3
Christopher's Perspective

The first day of school is complete and I'm waiting for Kennedy, so we can walk home. Unfortunately, our last classes of the day are not the same. She has to walk from the other side of the building to meet me. I'm just glad there wasn't any more drama during the school day because I don't know if I could have taken anymore. The first day of school started out with me having a fight with a dope fiend and that had me on edge all day long. I'm just ready to get back to the crib and kick back.

I'm standing on the corner of Milford Ave. waiting for my sister while I talk to a couple of guys in my class. We're talking about some girls in our grade that were looking good today. We have plans in the future to make moves on them. We all agree that there are seemingly more good-looking girls this year than in years past. In our minds, we're going to get all of them, but realistically we'll be lucky to get one or two of them. I mention to them that I put in some applications for work at a couple spots and I'm looking forward to hearing back from them.

One of the guys in the conversation mentions that he's going to put in some applications too. We discuss our optimism for the future, but the other guy in the conversation throws me off a bit. He's totally opposed to working a job while in high school. I don't see what the problem is with having a job in high school and I'm going to stick with my plan. I want to pick his brain some more about this, but my sister finally walks over to us. I dap my two classmates up and my sister and I start walking home.

My sister tells me that her last period class was cool and nothing eventful happened. That's good to hear because there's seemingly always something going on. We leave the school premises and walk down the hill on Bigelow Ave. to the corner store on Elizabeth Ave. because Kennedy wants some chips and a drink. As we approach the corner store, we see several people congregated on the corner in front of the store.

We stop walking toward the store and visually investigate what may be going on. We want to be sure that we're not walking into a harmful situation. The last thing we need is to walk into the middle of a gang fight or shootout. After a few seconds of peering at the few people gathered together, we realize that nothing ominous is transpiring, so we proceed to the store. We can tell that the guys gathered on the corner are all looking down at something. I surmise that they're rolling 'C lo', but we don't hear anyone shouting like normal during a dice game. Also, it's broad daylight and I've never seen anybody roll dice on this corner before.

"No, I don't think it's a dice game because no one is bent over and I can't see any money on the ground. I think they're looking at that bike," Kennedy says.

I reply, "I think you're right. I'm glad they aren't shooting dice because you know how dice games sometimes end."

"I know right. Somebody usually ends up beat up or shot up. The last thing we need is another body out here in Brick City. I'm really just tired of the drama. For real, for real," Kennedy voices.

I utter, "Right, then the block will be hot as hell for the next few weeks and I definitely ain't trying to be questioned by the police about what I've seen or heard."

We make it to the store and walk past the group of guys. It turns out that they are looking at the bike. I can't even deny the fact that the bike is dope. I don't think I've ever seen a bike as fresh as that. I hope someone isn't dumb enough to leave that bike unattended because it'll be snatched with the quickness. People out here aren't playing any games.

Kennedy words, "That bike is lit as fuck Chris! That joint is a Mercedes Benz bike. I saw the name printed on the frame of the bike. I thought that Mongoose that Brandon had was fire, but it ain't got shit on that bike outside."

"Son, I peeped that too. That shit is crazy! I almost wanna ask whoever owns the bike if I can see it, but I'm not though. We'll end up in a fight out here," I speak.

"Bruh, you better not ask him if you can look at his bike. You know if you even look at that bike, he'll assume that you're scheming on it. You know he'll say something sideways and then you'll have to beat his ass. No need to even go there," Kennedy suggests.

"That's real shit though. I'm not gonna mention it; I'll just keep it pushing when we leave out of here. I won't even look at that shit," I verbalize.

My sister gets her chips and drink and we walk to the register. I pay for her stuff and we leave. When we walk outside, the group of dudes are all gone. There's no trace of them whatsoever. We wonder if the cops ran them off the block while we were inside the store. It wouldn't be unusual for the police to rundown on the block and kick people off of it. What is unusual is that the bike that my sister and I were marveling about is still leaned up against the store.

"Yo, somebody lost their damn mind or

something. Ain't no way that somebody was dumb enough to leave their bike out here. That's some other shit! They must not know where we're at," I vocalize.

"No, that's really dumb as fuck! That bike will be gone in 2.5! We were the only ones in the store, so the person didn't even leave it outside while they went in the store. That's crazy," Kennedy acknowledges.

While we're walking up the block, we see Mark who's a dude from school. We stop and chat for a minute and we tell him about the bike that somebody left outside of the store. We speak so highly of the bike that he wants to see it for himself. It's almost like he doesn't believe us. All three of us walk back toward the store. Mark looks at the bike in amazement just as my sister and I did. Mark even decides to sit on the bike because it's so fresh.

"When we first got to the store there were like six dudes looking at the bike. We figured the bike belonged to one of them, but when we came out they were all gone, but the bike was still here. Shit, we just kept walking. We ain't fooling with that bike," I narrate.

Mark replies, "Son, you bugging! This bike is dope as hell. I'm about to take this shit. Somebody got caught slipping. I'm not leaving this bike sitting here. It probably belongs to somebody who's visiting from out of town and doesn't know how we get down in Brick City."

Kennedy chimes in, "Ain't no way anyone is that dumb. You better get off that bike and leave it right where it is. Taking that bike is bad dope for real!"

Kennedy grabs me by the arm and starts pulling me up the block in the direction of home. She wants no parts of Mark stealing the bike. She thinks that he's out of his mind. I tell Mark that I'll see him tomorrow at school and we walk up the hill. I don't think it's a good idea for Mark to swipe the bike either, but he's going to do what he wants to do. As we walk up the hill, Kennedy talks negatively about Mark's decision to take the bike. Ten seconds later Mark is riding the bike in the middle of the street. He looks over at us as he pops a wheelie on the bike. Kennedy and I just shake our heads as Mark speeds up Bigelow Ave.

"Mark, you better put that bike back. You don't know whose bike that is," I yell.

Mark waves me off and continues riding. The bike is dope, but Mark should be concerned that someone is going to come looking for it. I know if that were my bike, I would have never taken my eyes off of it. If I did manage to let a bike of that caliber get stolen, I'd comb every block looking for it. I'd be beyond livid to say the least. We get to the light on the corner of Milford and Bigelow Avenues and wait for the light to change.

While we're standing here waiting, we see several cars speed out from parking spaces on

Bigelow and Milford Avenues. Simultaneously, we see the police lights flashing and now their sirens are blaring and engines are roaring. We've seen this scene unfold a million times, so we know that the police are after someone. They must have been staking out a drug deal and now they're going to arrest the perpetrator. My sister and I don't move from our spot on the corner even though the light has changed for us to walk across the street.

We don't know which way these cop cars are going, so we wait to see where they're headed. The last thing we need is to start walking across the street and get ran over by one of the speeding cop cars. To our surprise, one of the unmarked cars attempts to cut off Mark's path. Mark realizes that they're after him for gaffling the bike. Mark decides not to give up. Instead of giving up, he takes the police on a chase. Mark jumps the curb while still on the bike and rides through the grass filled area on Milford Ave.

One of the officers who's further down the block, exits his car and attempts to grab Mark on foot. However, his efforts are to no avail because he falls while running after Mark. I don't know if it's Mark or the bike, but he's moving very fast on that bike. One of the police officers realizes that a foot chase is not going to work, so he jumps the curb in his car and pursues Mark through the grassy area. Mark is peddling and maneuvering that bicycle as if he's an Olympic cyclist competing for gold and someone's trying to overtake his lead.

My sister and I both agree that the cops are exerting a tremendous amount of energy and effort to catch Mark. He clearly has done something much worse than steal that bike. I'm glad I don't kick it with him heavily because I could have been caught up in his drama. The police have pretty much blocked off the direction Mark is riding in, so he turns and rides to Elizabeth Ave. and tries to cross the street to elude the police, but the traffic is too heavy for him to cross. As he slows down in attempt to cross the street, the police closes in on him. When he notices that they've gotten closer to him, he abandons his attempt to cross the street and starts riding back in our direction.

"He must have drugs on him because he's trying too hard to get away and the police are trying too hard to catch him," Kennedy voices.

"Yo, he definitely did something besides take that bike. I don't know what he was into, but it had to be something crazy for them to be after him like that," I offer.

"Right, that's why I don't keep a lot of people in my company because you never know what shady shit they're into," Kennedy speaks.

"You know how we do. Keep the circle mad tight. That's the only way to live out here. Shit, we can't trust everybody. Really, you're like the only person I truly trust. Like, I know you have my back always and no matter what," I verbalize.

"Of course, and I know you have mine," Kennedy says.

I voice, "I can't believe that the police are letting this play out for as long as they are. I've seen them end car chases much quicker than this before. They're chasing Mark back and forth for nothing."

"I was thinking the same damn thing. Really Mark should just give up because he's not getting away from them. It's just too many cops," Kennedy replies.

Mark is back on Bigelow zooming up the hill on the bike when a cop car pulls up beside him. The cop pulls out his gun and orders Mark to get off the bike and get on the ground. Mark decides to comply. He gets off the bike in the middle of the street and rests flat on his stomach. The cops block the street with their cars, so nobody can enter the block. The cop who tried to apprehend Mark on foot is the one who cuffs Mark. While he's on the ground, he's given several blows by the officers. It's foul that they're doing him like that because he's completely given himself up. They're clearly upset that he made them chase him and made them look foolish.

"Why'd you steal that bike?" one of the arresting officers asks.

Mark answers, "I didn't steal the bike. I don't know what you're talking about. One of my friends told me that I could borrow the bike. I was just borrowing it. I was bringing it back to him later."

The cop asks, "Is that right? Well, where's your friend now?"

Mark answers, "Yeah, that's right. He's over there on the corner with his sister. His name is Chris. He'll tell you everything."

My sister and I can hear everything that he's saying to the cops, but we don't know why he's telling him those things. Mark has to know that I'm not cosigning anything he just told them. We told him not to touch that bike, but he didn't listen to us. My sister and I are still confused because the cops still haven't mentioned anything other than Mark swiping the bike. We were sure that there was another reason for them going so hard to catch him. Damn, here comes the cops to talk to us.

"Hi, I'm Detective Johnson. I have a couple of questions to ask you. You two aren't in any trouble, but I need you to be honest and fully answer my questions," he says.

He asks us what school we go to, how we know Mark, and several other nonsense questions. We answer those questions without hesitation in hopes that he'll quickly let us go home. Honestly, we hate talking to the police because we know that talking to them could get us into trouble in our neighborhood. Next, he asks us what we know about the bike that Mark stole. Kennedy and I tell him that we have no affiliation with that bike whatsoever. I further tell him that the bike was posted at the corner store when we went in it not too long ago.

The cop believes our story over what Mark told them. Mark is within an earshot of our conversation with the cop and is mad that I didn't cover for him. I wasn't going to throw my sister and me under the bus because he's a dumb ass. We told him not to fool with the bike from the very beginning, but he made his own move and now he has to suffer the consequences of his actions. It's not our fault. The cop walks Mark over to us.

"We know you're lying Mark. They never told you that you could borrow that bike. You just made that up to save your ass," Officer Johnson speaks.

Mark responds, "I'm not lying. I promise you I'm telling the truth. On everything, Chris said it was his bike and that I could borrow it. I didn't know it wasn't really his bike."

Kennedy is heated by the lies that Mark's telling. She starts hurling curse words at him and even tries to get at him, but I grab her and tell her to calm down. I tell the cop one more time that Mark is telling falsehoods. He shares some shocking information with us that totally disproves Mark's lies. The cop tells us that the cops put the bike there to see if anyone would try to steal it. Also, they have the bike equipped with a listening device, so they overheard all conversations that were had within thirty feet of the bike. Mark is clearly on tape stating that he was taking the bike even though we warned against him doing so.

"This is retarded. Y'all must be bored as hell! You did way too much for a punk ass bike. It's a stolen bike. That's not even a real charge. Shit, I think you should just let me go home. There's no point in locking me up," Mark charges.

"We know you don't think it's a big deal, but it really is. You have broken the law. That bike is worth thirty-five hundred dollars. You've committed a felony by taking that bike. That's not petty theft even though you view it as only stealing a bike," Officer Johnson contends.

We talk for a few more minutes and then the cops let us go. Unfortunately, they do not let Mark go. They're taking him away in their car. He's going to be charged for the theft. My sister and I cross the street and head to the house. We are dumbfounded about the entire fiasco with the bike and Mark lying on me. This whole situation could have been avoided, but it wasn't. We discuss it on the way home.

REFLECTION

Sadly, this scenario is a real one. It's happening to people all over the place. People steal bikes and cars all the time and I don't think it's right. No one should steal anyone else's property. If it's not yours, you shouldn't take it. That philosophy works in many, if not most, circumstances. Unfortunately, there are some situations where a "no stealing philosophy" is non-existent. The situation where no stealing and other societal norms are abolished is when poverty is at play.

When people are submerged in poverty stricken environments, their needs trump all other things. The need to eat and have shelter become the motivating factors in their lives. Rules and regulations fall by the waist side in instances when your needs aren't being met. It's not likely that someone who hasn't eaten in a day is going to pass up a chance to get a meal or money for a meal when it presents itself. If the opportunity to eat, which means to survive, comes from stealing a pocketbook or a bike, the poverty-stricken person will seize the chance.

The symptoms of poverty are not a mystery. They can be diagnosed just as the symptoms of diabetes can be charted. Essentially, poverty is a disease and should be treated as such. Unfortunately, poverty isn't treated as a disease, but instead is seen as a criminal issue. Many will ask the question why is poverty treated as a criminal activity as opposed to an epidemic. It seems that poverty is treated as criminal because it impacts many black and Latino citizens.

We know that poverty adversely impacts the homes that people live in. Also, poverty negatively impacts access to healthy meals and adequate healthcare just to name a couple. We all know that having food is an essential item to maintain life. Additionally, people who live in poverty have behavioral problems. With that being said, there's no reason why poverty should be treated criminally, but it is.

In the instance of planting a bike outside a store is baiting someone to steal it. We know that a bike left unclaimed can be sold for money. If I'm a teenager who has hunger pains because I haven't eaten in days, I'm going to steal the bike and attempt to sell it for a few dollars. When the person in need sees the bike left unattended, he or she is not thinking about right and wrong. However, they are imagining themselves eating a fulfilling meal after they sell the merchandise. The need to survive supersedes everything else.

The law enforcement who places the bike at that specific location clearly knows that they are baiting anyone who sees it and suffering from the influences of poverty. We know this because of the shows that have the word "bait" in their titles. If you set out bait long enough, someone or something is going to take the bait. For example, if a person goes fishing, they have to bait their fishing rods. The hope is to entice a fish to take the bait and then they can reel it in.

They will capture their target if the bait stays long enough. Basically, when law enforcement places these bait items at convenience stores or liquor stores, they are targeting the people in that community. The cops know that these places are highly trafficked areas in the hood, so they focus on these areas to increase their chances of catching someone. It's a very meticulous and calculated plan they implement. The strategies the cops employ in these situations are the same as when hunters hunt animals in the woods.

If you're hunting bears, you'll need to know several things about bears. You'll need to know what they eat, where they congregate, what their footprints look like and what stimulates them among other things. At the point when you know those things, you can begin to hunt them. It will be simple because if you know enough about the bears, they'll come to you.

This is essentially the same thing as when the police did the stakeout of the bike they placed on the corner. Once you take the bait they set, they pounce on you and lock you up. Many people in the hood feel like they are being targeted and they are. Unfortunately, it's worse than being targeted because they're being hunted for profit and sold into privatized prison systems. It's no different than capturing animals in the wild and selling them to zoos and circuses.

The sad part is that if the bike wasn't put there, the bike wouldn't have been able to be stolen. The police in that instance created the environment for a crime to be committed and then locked Mark up for it. If you think about what entrapment means, this is clearly the definition of it. People in poverty are being lured into situations to commit crimes by the police and then being prosecuted for them. This is the reason people in poverty feel like law enforcement is against them. There's a distrust that has been created and perpetuated.

The police operate under the ruse that the point of this particular operation is to reduce theft in the area. Well, if that's the case, their approach is severely problematic. For one, it doesn't make sense to create the potential for crime and then charge people for doing exactly what you set them up to do. Also, the bikes that the cops use to entice disadvantaged people are bikes that cost thousands of dollars. Why is the price of the bicycle important? The reason the price is important is because the value of the item stolen changes the type of charge that the offender could receive. The dollar value of the bike is the difference between the crime being a felony or a misdemeanor. Your life can be harshly impacted because you stole a bike that the police set you up to steal in the first place. If you're over the age of 18, you can potentially carry a felony conviction with you that may prevent you from getting a high paying job.

With that being the case, many will challenge if the true motive is to reduce theft in the area. It's not likely that theft will be reduced because the poverty situation remains. Now, if the goal is to reduce theft, there's a better way to get it done. Those government resources can be used in a better fashion. For example, those bait bikes cost thousands of dollars. The money for those bikes could be used to have after school programs to educate kids or to feed them. The money that the police make to sit in vans and stakeout bikes being stolen could also be used to go into some type of child enrichment programs. These things would be much more beneficial to the communities they serve than paying officers to sit in vans and plot on community members who they know have an inclination to commit crimes. If you change the mind, you change the man!

What's even more troubling is that you don't see such a concentrated effort to lock up any other race in the country. If there's a problem within white America, the goal is to solve the problem not to lock the victims up. The narrative that is told is that black people are lower class citizens. The media presents these stories and television shows of us stealing things that white America wouldn't steal. They ask the question: Why would anyone steal a bike or shoplift? I ask why is white America not targeted. I would like to see television shows that target people who work on Wall Street. The government should set traps for people on Wall Street that involve them having the potential to make millions from insider trading tips. When they take the tips and try to use them, I'd like to see them get prosecuted. Let's bring balance to an unbalanced equation.

A moment ago, I mentioned that when a problem hits white America, the goal is to fix the problem and not to lock up the victims of the problem. Well, the evidence of that is blatant in the way government officials are approaching the predicament that white America is facing today. The problem I'm referencing the opioid addiction that's plaguing the nation. Many white people are finding themselves overdosing from opioid abuse at an extremely high rate, while other races haven't had a major change in the rate they're overdosing. As stated above, government officials want to end this problem immediately. They're not treating this drug abuse problem as a criminal act as crack-cocaine abuse was treated when black people were the abusers.

However, the country is calling this predicament an epidemic. Apparently, the users of opioids don't need to be jailed, but instead, they need to be rehabilitated. No one is calling for drug pushers to be jailed as they were when it negatively impacted black people. I have yet to hear the opioid addiction of white people be called a criminal offense. Surprisingly, I have heard terms such as, "America's Nightmare" used to refer to this problem. Somehow, when white America has a problem, it becomes the problem of the country as a whole.

Where are all the videos of federal agents kicking the doors in of the neighborhood guys who are pushing these drugs? We have yet to see this happen, but when black people abused crack in the eighties and nineties, we saw countless videos of this happening. This is not happening because what's happening to white America isn't seen as a criminal offense, but it is construed as a public health crisis.

Law makers want to stop the problem at the source. They know that it would be pointless to go after every street level person who's dealing opioids, so government officials are going all the way to the top. The opioid addiction for white America has gotten so bad that law makers have filed lawsuits against pharmaceutical companies because they feel they're culpable in the rise in drug overdoses that white America is experiencing.

As I stated above, when a problem hits white America, the goal is to get rid of the problem at its source and we can clearly see that's what they want to do with the opioid addiction and overdosing. Where was this level of concern for the health of American citizens when it was black people struggling with drug overdose and addiction? Why was it not a public health epidemic as it is now? Is it because black people aren't seen as important as white people? Unfortunately, I would have to answer "yes" to that.

CHAPTER 4
Christopher's Perspective

The first week of school is a wrap! The week didn't fly by as fast as I hoped it would, but either way it's over. I hope the amount of drama that popped off this week isn't indicative of how the rest of the school year is going to be. I can't endure an entire year worth of nonsense like this week has had. My week was ridiculous. I spent the rest of the week defending myself against accusations of being a snitch. Mark has been spreading rumors that I dimed him out to the police about the stolen bike incident even though he knows that it's not true. I've been told by numerous people that when they release Mark from juvenile detention he's going to beat me up. I find it funny how doing the right thing can still put a person in an adverse situation. This is another reason why it's so difficult to do the supposed right thing. It seems there's a negative outcome no matter what I do.

Well, the weekend is here and I'm going to focus on the football game tonight against Linden High School. The game is in their home stadium, so my sister, her homegirl, and I are going out there. Linden is supposed to be really good this year, but we're confident that we're going to get the dub. The guys on our team have been hyped up all day about the game and assure us that their energy is going to translate into a win for us.

We leave school and start walking towards the house when my sister and I start getting messages on The Gram. A lot of students from our school are stating that they're going to the game in Linden tonight. The plan is for everybody to leave Newark to head to Linden at 5:30. We plan to meet at a McDonald's on St. George's Ave. in Linden before the game. The McDonald's is only a few minutes from the stadium where the game will be played. It's going to be lit tonight.

Kennedy and I go home to chill for a little while and to change clothes before the game. There are a lot of good looking girls from Linden and I plan to scoop one up while we're out there, so I'm putting forth extra effort for my outfit to be lit. My sister is showering and changing clothes too. Just as we both finish getting dressed, my sister's friend pulls up outside to take us to the game. Her older brother let her borrow his car, so we could hit the game up. The car's a hooptie, but it works well enough to get us to the game.

We jump on route 1&9 to head to Linden. On the way to the Linden, I receive a text from one of my friends telling me that Mark got released from juvie not too long ago. I'm glad he's been released, but I really don't have a dog in his fight. I don't want to see anyone in jail. I respond to his text casually and don't say anything too in depth. We get off the highway and take some back streets through Linden. We drive past Saint Marks Park on the way to McDonald's. I was at this park when they filmed one of the And One Basketball Mixtapes a while back.

Finally, we pull up to McDonald's. Surprisingly, many of our classmates have already made it here. Normally, everybody's late even though they say they're going to be on time. We get inside and order our food. There are so many people from our school in here that it seems like we're at lunch in the school cafeteria. The mood is light and jovial and everyone's having a good time. Everyone's posting live videos on IG and Snap. As always, somebody has to attempt to kill the atmosphere. Mark just went live on IG and is telling every one of his followers that he's going to fuck me up when he sees me and that they shouldn't chill with me because I'm a rat. He's chanting that snitches get stitches and he's calling rounds on me.

Mark states via Instagram, "It's an on sight

when I see you nigga! On everything, I'm gonna make you see blood when I pull up on you bitch nigga. That was some real bitch shit you did. I'm popping off in 2.5 boy!"

As high school students often do, they're trying to hype me up to respond to Mark's threats. Several of them are telling me to respond back to him with a live video of my own. They must not know me very well. The one thing I won't do is add fuel to an already volatile situation. I feel he can say whatever he wants as long as he doesn't put his hands on me. I will not allow anyone to violate my personal space or physically harm me.

I've never understood how people go back and forth with people verbally. I have bigger and better things to do with my time. Besides, people always have something negative to say, so if you respond to all of them, you'll be spending a vast majority of your days in conflict. Many of those verbal conflicts will then turn into physical altercations. That means that a person could be fighting a couple times a week. We all know high school is filled with immaturity and everyone's trying to prove themselves to their peers. I choose to be above the drama and only prove things to myself.

We leave McDonald's and head to the game. The ride is only a few minutes long and the only thing my sister's friend wants to talk about is the fake beef between me and Mark. I call it a fake beef because it's not a real conflict. I don't have a problem with Mark at all. I'm good with the situation. I'm calm and not all worked up like everyone was over at McDonald's. They want me to step out of my character because he called rounds on me.

I'm not opening my mouth about the situation at all. My plan is to keep quiet about it and not add fuel to the fire. In my opinion, Mark is looking for a real reason to brawl with me. I can't ignore the possibility that Mark is really going to be reckless enough to try to fight me. I don't want to fight him, but I'll be ready for him if he tries me. Where I'm from, you know better than to be caught slipping. Additionally, if I don't do much to agitate the situation, he may underestimate me. My silence may cause him to think that I'm afraid and incapable of beating him. He's my potential enemy, so there's no reason to let him know what I'm thinking.

We make it to Linden's football field after walking a few blocks. Unfortunately, there weren't any close parking spaces to the stadium. We walk along the fence of the football stadium and can see that there's a sea of people inside the game. I can tell from all of the orange and black attire that most of the people we see are here in support of Linden. Linden High School's mascot is a tiger and their colors are orange, black, and white, so it's fitting that those are the majority of the colors we see.

To our dismay, the line to get into the game is quite long. While we wait on line, we link back up with some of our classmates who were in McDonald's. Some are complaining about the long ticketing line while others want to talk to me about Mark. I stay true to form and don't feed into their bullshit.

"What you gonna do bruh?" my classmate Kendall asks.

I immediately ask back, "Do bout what?"

"About Mark. He's telling everybody that you ratted on him and that he's gonna fuck you up when he sees you. He's been popping off all over Instagram for the last few hours about it. I know you've heard about it by now," Kendall reports.

I reply, "Oh, I heard about that, but he's not serious. He's just playing with all of his Instagram followers. That ain't bout nothing."

Kennedy replies, "That's dead Kendall. It ain't even that serious. I don't know why everybody's hyping the nonsense up. Ain't nobody fighting."

"True, well as long as you know what Mark is saying. I didn't want him to run up on you and you not know anything about it," Kendall speaks.

I voice, "Son, good looking out on that! I appreciate it, but I'm good over here. Ain't nothing happening like I said."

We end that conversation and finally make it inside the game. We walk through the Linden side of the game to see if I can get a glimpse of some of their female students. My sister and her friend walk a few feet ahead of me, so they don't cramp my style. I see several cute girls, but I don't immediately move on them. We make it through the Linden side of the field and walk over to the away side. I sit in the bleachers with some of my associates from school while my sister and her friend continue to stroll around the stadium.

The game starts and I'm locked into it. I know we can beat Linden if we focus and execute. My game watching is interrupted several times by people who want the scoop on whether I'm going to fight Mark or even respond to his threats. Even though it's not easy, I continue not to respond and downplay everything. I can tell by their reactions that they aren't happy with my reluctance to give them anything to run with, but I'm okay with that. It's really not any of their business anyway.

Halftime arrives relatively fast and I'm thirsty. I decide to walk to the concession stand to grab a drink. Hopefully, I can bump into some of those lit Linden girls I saw earlier. That'll be dope if I get a couple of their Snaps and can keep in contact with them. I make it to the concession stand and end up back with my sister and her friend. I should've known that they'd be over here. My sister always hits the concession stand during halftime intermissions.

I tell my sister to get me a water and walk away from her. I would have stayed with them, but I see one of the Linden girls I saw in the stands. I know we made eye contact earlier when I walked past, so I have to see if she's interested because I surely am interested in her. I walk directly over to her and speak.

"Hi, my name's Chris. I saw you when I first walked in the game and your warm smile and dimples caught my eye. I couldn't speak then, so here I am now," I orate.

"Thank you. My name is Aliyah. I caught a glimpse of you too. I guess you couldn't speak cause you were with your lil girlfriend. I saw you when you first came in and when you walked through the Linden side of the game," Aliyah utters.

I swiftly clear up the confusion, "Nah, that was my twin sister and her friend. I don't have a girlfriend, but if you act right, it could be you. If you don't believe me, we can walk over to her now. She's getting me a bottle of water."

"You good! I was just playing with you, but how do you know that I would wanna be your girlfriend? I don't know you like that," Aliyah responds.

I verbalize, "I know because I'm gonna treat you the way you wanna be treated and I ain't gonna shit on you. Plus, I'm just likable and you're gonna fall for me."

"Is that right? You think you're all that?" Aliyah asks.

"Yeah, that's right. No, I don't think I'm all

that, but I know what I bring to the table. I don't play no games and don't be on that bullshit," I answer.

"Well, that's good cause y'all lil boys be playing too many games," Aliyah states.

"See, that's your problem. You're used to dealing with lil boys, but I'm on some grown man shit. I'm nothing like the normal," I say.

I have Aliyah walk with me towards Kennedy, so I can get my water. I introduce the two of them and then me and Aliyah walk around the stadium while we talk. She seems to have a good head on her shoulders and has mad jokes. That's great to me that she jokes a lot because I love to joke and laugh too. She's in the same grade as me and shares some of the same interests with me. We stop walking for a little while and watch some more of the game. It's a great game and the score is tied up in the fourth quarter.

Shabazz has the ball and is driving down the field. Aliyah is mad that her team may lose and I'm happy. I'm teasing her and she's talking junk back to me. According to Aliyah, there's no way Linden is losing the game. I beg to differ with her. It's crazy to me how we connected at this game. I haven't looked at another girl since we linked up. Shabazz scores a touchdown on the drive, but misses the extra point. Linden has the ball back and now has a shot to do their thing. Aliyah is hyped up and cheering her team on. I don't say too much because we're on the Linden side of the stadium and I don't want to piss someone off.

Moments later, my phone starts going crazy. I'm getting back to back messages on Snap and Instagram. I know there has to be some nonsense going on for my phone to be going crazy. I decide not to answer the messages because I don't want to be rude to Aliyah. Next, my sister calls my phone. When I see her name pop up, I answer it immediately. When I answer the call, I hear people shouting in the background.

"Yoyo," I say.

Kennedy inquires, "Where are you?"

"I'm on the Linden side of the game chilling," I answer.

"Well, Mark is in the game acting like he's gonna beat me up if you don't come over to where we are," Kennedy replies.

"You serious? Where you at?" I inquire angrily.

Kennedy answers, "I'm on the Shabazz side right where we were sitting before. It's like a million people over here now. Just look for the crowd of people."

"Aight, I'll be there in a minute. I'm coming now. It's always some bullshit," I say as I hang up.

When I make that comment, Aliyah wants to know what's going on, but I don't have the time to tell her. I just let her know that I have to go back to the Shabazz side of the field now. She decides that she's going to walk with me. Part of me doesn't want her to go over there with me because I don't want her to see me arguing and potentially fighting. They say that first impressions are everything and I don't want her first impression of me to be marred by a physical altercation. Aliyah may think that I'm a wanna be thug or something. Either way, I have no choice, but to make sure my sister is safe. I can't let Mark hurt her on account of me.

It seems like it takes us forever and a day to get over to my sister even though it doesn't. Fortunately, by the time we make it over there, the crowd has dispersed. A few cops, who are providing security for the game, saw the large crowd and broke it up. My sister fills me in on everything that Mark was saying to her. He claims that if I keep ducking him that he's going to beat my sister up instead. I don't get why we can't just chill sometimes. Why does everything have to be about beef?

I know one thing and it's that I won't be leaving my sister's side while we're at this game. In fact, I'm thinking we should just bounce now. The outcome of the game is really irrelevant at this point. Being safe is the most important thing. I tell Kennedy and her friend that we should leave now. Of course, Kennedy agrees with me, but her friend does not. She wants to stay to see the outcome of the game and to hangout a little longer. Unfortunately, we rode with her, so we have no choice, but to wait with her. My head is on a swivel for sure.

I continue chopping it up with Aliyah. Kennedy and Aliyah are getting along very well too. The game is still tight and very exciting. Linden scored a touchdown to tie the game and are about to kick the extra point. I want Shabazz to win the game, but I want to leave even more, so I'm hoping that Linden makes the extra point when they kick it. We'll just have to wait and see what happens. There's no time on the clock, so if he makes it, the game will be over. The kicker kicks the ball and it goes directly through the upright. Linden has won the game and now we can skate out of here.

I hope Mark is gone by now. The last thing we need is to have a fight out here in Linden. We could get locked up and have to sit in a Linden jail. Who wants that? I know I don't. The referees are making an announcement. Apparently, the game isn't over. Shabazz's coach called a timeout right before Linden snapped the ball, so the kick doesn't count. A lot of people don't know that the game isn't over and continue to exit. A pretty big chunk of the crowd has left and I'm really hoping Mark is gone.

Linden re-kicks the ball and the outcome is no different from the first attempt. The kick is good and the game is over. Linden has won the game. I get Aliyah's contact information and she dips back to the Linden side of the game to catch up with her friends. Kennedy, her friend, and I head to the exit, so we can go home. I'm looking at everyone with intense scrutiny. Every time I hear a loud scream, I assume it's Mark running up on me. I'm really on ten about this situation and I hate this feeling. We get outside the stadium after a long wait and beeline for the car. We make it to the car without incident.

Just as I reach for the door, Kennedy screams, "Watch out!"

Without really knowing what I'm watching out for, I duck, turn, and swing. I'm glad I chose correctly because Mark is swinging at me. I was able to connect with my punch and it made him stumble backwards. Kennedy gets out of the car and is watching intensely. A few other people from our school are watching. They obviously knew what Mark was up to beforehand. It would have been nice of them to warn me, but that may be too much to ask. They're not my friends anyway. My only true friend is my sister.

I fully turn around to face Mark. I decide not to rush him while he's stumbling backwards. I don't want any unfair advantages for this fight. I put my guard up and prepare for this unwanted fight. Many people are recording the fight, but I'm tuning them out. Mark starts hurling curses at me and screaming threats. He has his guard up and promises that he's going to beat my ass. I don't respond and just keep my guard raised.

A random person supporting Mark screams, "Fuck him up!"

Mark bounces around in a boxing cadence and comes toward me. I don't move an inch. Mark throws a wild punch at me and I slip it easily. After I dip the punch, I punch him in the jaw. He staggers back and I rush him. I hit him two more times in the face and grab him around his neck. He gets out of my grip and attempts to grab my legs to slam me, but I prevent that. When he ducks his head to take control of my legs, I knee him in the face and he falls to the ground. I stand over him and punch him in his face several more times. Once he stops fighting back, I stop hitting him and walk off.

"Kennedy, get in the car!" I scream.

Kennedy and her friend get in the car and we pull off. My hands are shaking profusely because my adrenaline is pumping. I start punching the back of Kennedy's seat. I'm beyond livid and hate that I had to fight. That's not my style and I abhor violence. I feel it should be avoided whenever possible. Unfortunately, there was no way I could have avoided the conflict because Mark brought it to me. I had to defend myself, but I know these types of situations normally escalate to other things. Now, I really have to watch my back.

REFLECTION

Not all situations can be avoided. Sometimes, people come at you and no matter what you do, you can't escape the situation. In many instances, the other person is the aggressor and won't stop until they get things off their chest. The best thing to do in a situation where someone is aggressively taunting you is to not add fuel to the fire. The best thing to do is to avoid the person at all costs. The person being taunted should never respond via social media either. The hope is that the aggressor eventually calms down and let's their issue go. Furthermore, it's in the best interest of the person being sought out to not gossip to other people about the incident because the gossip will eventually make it back to the aggressor. Unfortunately, this doesn't always quell the issue, so you may have to eventually resort to engaging in physical combat.

CHAPTER 5
Christopher's Perspective

The video of me beating Mark up has been shared and viewed countless times. Most people my age would love seeing themselves winning a fight, but not me. Everyone's in my DMs giving me props for a pointless fight. I don't want kudos for anything negative. I only want to be applauded for positive and upstanding occurrences. That's the only way to bring esteem to myself, my family, and my city. Winning that fight against Mark really isn't a big deal because I've spent some time boxing in a real gym.

I had Mark beat from the time he threw his hands up. I don't tell people that I go to the gym to box from time to time because I don't want to put a target on my back. Once people know you're good at something, everybody wants to try you. I'm definitely not with that. Besides, I'm pretty modest and I'm not a braggart. I don't like extra attention, so flying under the radar works best for me.

We stop at Wendy's on the way home from the game to grab a four for four. We make it back to Brick City to go home. We pull up to our block only to see several cop cars in front of the house. The police lights are highly visible in the dark of the night. Unfortunately, the cops being here doesn't raise any alarm for us. The cops being here is a common occurrence. The only thing we never know is what time they're coming. The guys who live in the units beside and above our apartment sell drugs, so there's never a dull or quiet moment here.

You never know who's going to show up. Most of the time it's just the fiends who traffic the house, but in other instances there are people who wish to cause the drug dealers harm. The drug dealers often have beef with other drug dealers and sometimes things spill over into violent altercations here at the crib. I've had a gun pulled on me twice by the rival drug dealers because they thought I was one of the drug dealers from next door or upstairs. The home is supposed to be a sanctuary; a place where you can relax and be comfortable, but often times, it's not. Instead, it's often chaotic and filled with tumult.

Sometimes I close my eyes tightly and hope to be somewhere else when I open them, but I never am. I'm still in the hood with seemingly no escape. I'm waiting on graduation day, so my sister and I can get out of here for good. Maybe, we'll go to a college out of state or something. Honestly, it can be in state just so long as it's out of the hood. I'm sure with these cops here it's business as usual.

We get out of the car and begin to approach the crib. The two cops standing on the porch are watching everyone who's outside of the apartment building. The cops don't stop us from entering the fence in front of our place because they recognize us as living in the building. They're here so much that they know who all of the tenants of the building are. It's so bad that they even know us by name.

Officer Blackwell asks, "What's up twins?"

"Nothing much," Kennedy responds.

I simply nod my head to the officers. I have a distrust of the police, so it's hard for me to interact with them. I feel like the head nod is enough. Kennedy doesn't trust them either, but she's just being cordial. We walk past the cops and enter the hallway and notice that it really is business as usual for the cops. Several of the guys who live in the building and some of their boys who live elsewhere are being detained in the hallway. They have all of them facing the wall with their hands tied behind their backs with plastic restraints. One cop has his gun drawn on them ensuring that they don't move.

We call it business as usual because the cops raid the crib about once a month and never lock anyone up. They detain the guys in the hallway and search all of their apartments for drugs and money. The problem is that they're dirty cops. What they're doing is robbing the drug dealers. When they find the money and drugs, they present both findings to the drug dealers. However, they don't lock the drug dealers up. Instead, the police officers keep the money and leave the drugs for the dealers to sell and get back on their feet and then like clockwork they come back the following month to do it all over again.

The drug dealers got smart and started hiding the money and drugs in the basement, but the cops got hip to that and continued with business as usual. In one regard, the cops are really doing them a favor by not locking the guys up, but on another front, the cops are benefiting from illegal activity on their part and the part of the drug dealers. I guess it wouldn't be possible if the guys weren't doing what they're doing to begin with.

Kennedy and I walk up the steps and go into our unit. We listen to the commotion in the hallway and talk about it for a while. We always wonder if the cops will ever stop doing this, but we both agree that it's not likely. Kennedy falls asleep on the couch, so I figure it's time for me to shut it down too. I can't even front like I'm not extremely tired. It's been a full day for me. I lie on the bed and fall into a coma-like slumber.

I wake up to my sister playing Rhianna's album very loudly. She makes good music, but my sister is like borderline in love with her. Rhianna's hot, but my sister is on stalker status. She's dancing around the house while she's eating some bacon and eggs. I go in the kitchen and notice that she made me some food too. I'm souped up because I'm starving.

"Chris, Jenaiya is having a cookout at like one o'clock. She told us to come through if we weren't doing anything later," Kennedy says.

"Word. You trying to go?" I ask.

Kennedy answers enthusiastically, "Bruh, it's probably gonna be lit! You know it's gonna be cold soon, so we can get in one last cookout before the weather changes. Plus, you know Jenaiya's aunt Audrey is doing a lot of the cooking like last time. Her food is bananas!"

"Yeah, it probably will be lit. You know if you wanna go, I'm going with you. Yo, I didn't know her aunt made the food last time. She definitely can cook," I reply.

Kennedy decides that we're going to Jenaiya's house for the cookout. It's still a few hours from now and it's only a few blocks from us, so I workout before we go. I love working out because it pumps me up and makes me feel good. I even get my sister to workout with me. She doesn't exercise very much, but she does focus on her abs. She has a myriad of stomach exercises that she does. After we finish exercising, I shadow box for a while. Kennedy goes and gets in the shower, so she can start getting ready to bounce. A little while later, Kennedy exits the shower and I go jump in.

I take my shower and start getting dressed. Kennedy is ready before me, so now she's rushing me. I don't know why she's rushing me because it's only a cookout and we don't have to be there on time. I thought females like to be fashionably late anyway. After thirty minutes of hearing Kennedy's mouth, I'm finally ready. We leave the crib and walk to Jenaiya's house. We arrive a little bit after two o'clock. Our timing on getting to the cookout is perfect because the first batch of food is just coming off the grill. That works for me because we get to get our plates before people start touching all over the food. Additionally, it'll be nice and hot.

The smell of the barbecued food infiltrates the afternoon air and entices my taste buds. I beeline straight toward the grill. While I'm at the grill waiting for some chicken, I see fish in the deep fryer. I'm definitely going to grab some fish when it's ready. I love fish when it's fresh out of the grease. I get the chicken off the grill and then go to the table and scoop up Jenaiya's aunt Audrey's fabulous potato salad and other side dishes that she's prepared. I take my sister her plate and grab her a drink out of the cooler and then I return to the grill, so I can get my food. It's only right that I fix my sister's plate and bring it to her. It's my responsibility to treat her like the queen she is and to set a standard for any guy who wants to date her to meet or exceed.

I prepare my food and then sit down with my sister. We eat our food in no time. We devour it because everything tastes so good. As I clear our trash from the table, I look over at the guy cooking the fish and I notice that he's taking the fish out. I practically run over to him to get a piece of fish. Kennedy motions for me to get her a piece too. As we eat the fish, more and more people arrive at the cookout. Fortunately, one of the people who just arrived is the DJ. He begins setting up his equipment.

It's thirty minutes later and the DJ is completely set up and has the music playing loudly. So far, he seems to know what he's doing on the tables because he hasn't played a wack song yet. My sister and I are just chilling at the table bopping our heads to the music. It seems like the neighborhood must be hearing the music because the cookout is becoming inundated with people. It was almost like the music summoned the people here. There are many of our classmates here as well as many people who are younger and older than us. Some of the people are family members of Jenaiya, while others are friends from the neighborhood.

The cookout is going smoothly. The DJ is now playing the "Cupid Shuffle" and everyone is up dancing. However, I'm not doing any line dancing. I'm just chilling watching my sister and everyone else dance. Kennedy has me on camera duty. She gave me the task of recording her dancing, so she can post it to her IG account. You'd think that she can't hold her own phone and record herself. I just laugh to myself as I record her doing her thing. The DJ plays several line dancing songs in a row. Both, the older people and younger people are enjoying the songs. This is the way cookouts are meant to be. The weather is perfect, the food is delicious, and everyone's having a good time. The best part of it all is that there's no drama.

After dancing to several line dancing songs, my sister and many others decide to call it quits. Many of the older people dancing are complaining about being tired and needing rest. My sister started to sweat a little too much for her comfort, so she sat down. The dance floor would have been cleared of the older people even if they hadn't gotten tired because the DJ just put on a song by Migos. There's no way that the older people would have danced to this song. "Bad and Boujee" is a hit with my age group, but most adults despise it. In fact, they despise pretty much all of the music my generation enjoys.

Now, the dance floor is completely dominated by teenagers and kids even younger than us. All of the kids are doing various dances that are current to our generation. Some of the older people here are watching them dance. One of the older women suggests that there should be a dance contest. Many of the kids become excited about the proposition. The dance contest begins with one little girl who's probably ten years old gyrating at a thousand miles per hour. Kennedy gives me a look of disgust and disapproval.

"Bruh, she's too young to be popping her ass like that. I'm just saying that's too much for her to be a little kid. Ain't no way," Kennedy says.

"Yo, you're reading my mind. I'm not even looking over there anymore. That's why I looked to the ground. I don't want to see that. It's pointless to watch," I reply.

Kennedy states, "I wonder where that little girl's mother is. I know she can't approve of that girl twerking her body like that. If she was my daughter, I'd yank her little ass off the dance floor right in front of everybody. I don't play like that."

"Sis, I already know what you'd do to her. I can picture you snatching her up. That's why I'm laughing so hard," I voice.

"Oh my goodness! And she's acting like she's right. Dat little girl doesn't know anything about anything, but she's over there shaking her booty. Well, shaking whatever she wants to call it. I'm too through right now," Kennedy verbalizes angrily.

Unfortunately, the dancing doesn't end here. It's just the beginning on the nonsense. When that girl finishes dancing, another one takes her place. She's basically doing the same motions that the girl before her did. I didn't think it'd be possible, but she's throwing her body parts around harder than the other little girl was. Kennedy is fuming to say the least. She doesn't like to see people not act their age. What's even more despicable is that the grownups at the cookout are egging these girls on. They're cheering louder and louder every time one of them pops their booty. Several people are videotaping them as they dance. Some of them are sending live feeds of the kids dancing to social media.

"This is not cute and I don't see how people are acting like there's nothing wrong with the spectacle. This is despicable and deplorable, but somehow, they're acting like it's all good. I'm not even the one dancing and they're not my kids, but I'm ashamed and embarrassed for them," Kennedy articulates.

REFLECTION

Now, dancing is a part of the culture that black people are a part of, so there's nothing foul about dancing. It seems to be in our DNA and is a celebratory act in most cases. Dancing is an expression of who we are and is a way that our people bond and share time together. Dancing should always be in the mix of things whenever we gather. However, there are some things that are problematic when it comes to the way we dance when we congregate.

The first thing that's problematic is in the dancing itself. Many of the dance moves that our culture uses involve gyrations and body movements that can be construed as sexual. For example, in some instances the dances entail a lot of booty thrusts that cause one's breasts to jiggle. Depending on the dance routine, there may even be instances when females will drop to the floor into a full split and bounce up and down. It's pretty much a sex simulation.

I don't think that there is a problem with adults doing these types of moves because they're grown and can do as they choose, but when it comes to kids, there is a problem. Children should be exempt from performing such body movements. It's despicable to see kids moving their bodies in manners that should be reserved for adults. Children need to be treated as what they are and not mimic actions of adults. Also, adults need to set the example for what proper decorum is and constantly remind children on what is and is not acceptable. The last thing anyone should do is cheer children on when they bounce their bodies around sexually.

Another aspect of dancing in our culture that I find to be troublesome is that there's an over representation of dancing at our gatherings. We all know that our people have more to offer to the world than just dancing, but the other things we bring to the table are not promulgated in the same fashion as dancing. How do we change this problem? The solution is really not complicated. The elders of the family have to set the example, so it starts with them. In order to bring balance to a family gathering, there should be activities that cater to many different things.

The first thing that should happen is that the family should join in a prayer. That will bring a level of solemnity to the gathering. It sets the tone for the function and brings everyone together and enables them to focus as a family. Everyone's on the same accord. The next step is to get to the purpose of the gathering. If the gathering is festive, then let the fun stuff begin, but there's a way to do that. There should be music and dancing, but that should not be absent of other artistic elements. For example, someone could read a poem that one of the family members wrote or even display a picture that one of the family members drew. The talent of the family can be showcased in the form of a family talent show or just as a display like in a museum for people to look at. These types of things celebrate the abilities of all family members and doesn't cater to just dancing.

Additionally, there should be a component of the family celebration that pays homage to education also. This can be accomplished in a manner that has the kids and adults pick a few black heroes who aren't normally discussed and give a short bio on them. Another thing that could be done is to have a spelling bee or trivia event. What adding these things will do show is the youth of the family that there's value and importance in things that are outside of dancing. The worst that could happen by doing this is that the family may become well-rounded and the youth may stumble on an interest in the arts that they never knew existed.

These things should not be done privately either. They should all be shared with others. People are quick to share pictures of them out for drinks or enjoying a tasty meal on social media, but don't show pictures of families in prayer. In many instances, social media is dominated by fight videos and other worthless representations, so it would be refreshing to make it known that families are doing other things. We all know black people can dance, but it's time to flaunt all of our abilities.

CHAPTER 6
Christopher's Perspective

Monday rolls back around seemingly quicker than normal. I mean, the weekend always shoots by quickly, but this weekend sailed by as if we skipped Sunday altogether. It's cool that the weekend shot past so fast because I like school a lot. However, I'm not really feeling the extra attention I've been receiving today. People haven't gotten over my fight with Mark. Unfortunately, the video is still circulating and some people are just seeing it for the first time. The more new people who see the video, bring a new interest as to what happened and is keeping the situation fresh. I wish I could scrub internet of the video completely and bury the incident, but I can't. Gladly, Mark hasn't taken to the internet to verbally assault me anymore. I'm hoping that the conflict is settled for him too.

We're only in first period and I've lost count of the number of people who have approached me about the fight. They've all seen the video and tell me that I have nice hands and that I should get into boxing. It's only a matter of time before somebody tries to fight me just to prove to everyone else that they can beat me. I don't play into the way I won the fight so convincingly and attribute my winning the fight to sheer luck. Of course, no one is buying my bullshit story. The video tells it all and my words don't refute what they saw in the video.

A lot of people are telling me that they never really liked Mark because he thinks he's all that and he runs his mouth too much. Furthermore, they're glad that I beat him up. Many of them tell me to let them know if Mark and I fight again because they want to be there to watch it live. I've even inadvertently assumed the name of Little Mayweather. I refuse to answer to that name, but my classmates seem to find it fitting. They've even gone so far as to hashtag the video clip with that name.

By the end of the block, the conversations about the fight are over. I didn't give my classmates the hype about the fight that they wanted me to, so they abandoned it. Also, my teacher redirected us to our work as she walked around monitoring our group work assignments. I decide not to stand in the hallway in between the end of first period and the beginning of second period because people may be talking about the fight. I get to second period early and complete the bell work assignment that the teacher has for us daily. I have everything I need for today's class out in front of me and I'm ready to work.

My sister makes it to class a couple of minutes after me. She hung out in the hallway talking to friends before she came in. I don't blame her because there's nothing wrong with it as long as you're on time and prepared to work when class starts. If I wasn't attempting to avoid the drama, I would've hung out for a moment myself. The bell hasn't sounded yet and my sister is approaching my desk. I'm slightly surprised that she's coming over to my desk because she never does that. When she's in class, she's all business and not a person who wastes time. Normally, when she enters classes we have together, she goes directly to her seat and gets out whatever materials are needed for that class and then completes any bell work.

"What's wrong?" I ask.

Kennedy replies, "Why does something have to be wrong? Why are you so paranoid all the time?"

"Sis, cut the bullshit. I know you just as well as you know me, if not better than you know me. Yo, you never come to my desk once you come through the door. You know that just like I do, so stop playing and tell me what's wrong," I answer.

Kennedy states, "Alright, you're right, but there's nothing really wrong, but Keerah told me that Mark is in school today. She said she saw him by the gym earlier. I just wanted to tell you, so you'd know just in case he tries to steal off on you again. That's it though, so ain't nothing really wrong Mister Know-it All."

I respond, "That's what's up. I figured he'd be back today or tomorrow. I'm surprised he didn't put it on social media that he's back at school. Chances are, he probably didn't want me to know, so he could get at me."

"Damn, I didn't think about it like that. You know he's normally loud as hell and boisterous, but not now. Shit, I was hoping it's because you beat his ass and he didn't want any more action, but you may be right," Kennedy voices.

"I would love to think that's the case, but you know how that goes. As soon as I think like that, is when he'll catch me slipping. I'm good though. Thanks for telling me, but go get ya bell work done. That's more important than talking about lame ass Mark. We have to stay focused," I verbalize. "I'm kinda tired of talking about it."

"Okay, I'm going, but if I hear something about him talking reckless or something, I'm going to tell you even if you don't want to hear it," Kennedy informs.

She goes to her seat and begins working. The class fills in and the bell rings. The teacher takes attendance while the class completes the bell work. Moments later, the teacher discusses the assignment with the class and transitions into her lecture. Next, she shows us a video that we have to take notes on. The video is playing and I find it extremely boring and useless, but nonetheless, I still stay awake and take the required notes on the video.

I survey the room and see that many people clearly find the video just as boring as I do because many of my classmates are fast asleep. Gladly, my sister isn't one of them. I would have had to wring her neck if she was asleep. After we take notes on the video, we will have to answer several questions. About twenty minutes later, the video finishes and the students who were sleeping start waking up. Not surprisingly, the ones who were sleep are clueless. They have no idea what the video was about and they also don't have any notes. The teacher explains the assignment and tells us that we can work with a partner and we can use our notes. Of course, Kennedy and I work together. I know and trust her work ethic and I'm never disappointed with her effort.

Kevin is one of the students who went to sleep during the video and has no notes. This isn't the first time he's fallen asleep in class. Unfortunately, it happens quite frequently with him. He's the star quarterback for our school and has several Division I colleges looking at him. He gets plenty of rest during the school day from what I understand. I know this is only an elective class, but you still have to be attentive and he's not. Now, he's looking for a partner to work with who has the notes.

Kevin asks, "Chris, you want to work with me today?"

"Nah, bruh I'm working with my sister. You know I always work with her when the teacher lets us choose our partners," I answer.

"Come on man. I fell asleep. Man, I think I saw the first few minutes of the video and then I was out. I don't know what that shit was about," Kevin reports.

I say, "I know you were sleep because I heard you snoring. Son, you were even drooling on the desk. I'm good though because I'm still working with my sister."

"Yo, I was tired as hell. That's why I went to sleep. Well, I didn't go to sleep; I actually fell asleep. There is a difference," Kevin speaks.

"True, but I went to sleep early last night, so I wouldn't be sleepy in school today. You bugging man. You shoulda took it down early too," I narrate.

Kevin articulates, "Shit, I wish I coulda went to sleep early, but I couldn't. I had football practice and then I had to meet with a recruiter. Son, by the time I got home it was late as hell. Wasn't nothing I could do differently to get to sleep early."

"I feel you, but you gotta get ya work done. If you don't sleep properly, you won't be able to even engage your work. That's why you fell asleep," I say.

Kevin shoots back, "Nah, you're wrong on that. I see it differently. The way I see it is if I went to sleep early last night, I wouldn't have been able to meet with the recruiter."

Kennedy voices her opinion, "School comes before sports though. You have to get your work done in order to play sports."

"No disrespect, but you're tripping. Look around you and tell me that you really believe that academics come before sports. I want you to tell me in what forum does education trump sports. I know as smart as you two are that you can't possibly believe that," Kevin charges.

"Well, I know for me that my education comes before sports, but I can't speak for everyone else," Kennedy says.

"Well, clearly society thinks differently. Since I've been playing football, I've been to countless pep-rallies. I'm talking about the entire student body packed into the gym screaming for the football team or the basketball team. The entire school day is altered or interrupted, so praise can be given to athletes in those instances. Shit, athletes even get out of class earlier than everyone else just to get prepared for the pep-rally," Kevin verbalizes.

"You definitely aren't lying. We see it all the

time. It really does seem like it's athlete first and then student," I reply.

"If I had a thousand dollars, I'd bet you that neither one of you have ever been to a pep-rally for something related to academics. You're lucky if you get to go to an academic banquet or something, but it's not nearly as celebrated as athletics are. Most people may not even know about the banquet. Thousands of people gather for sporting events, but you'll never see thousands of people at a debate team match. Nobody cares about that stuff and that's why I dump all of my effort into football. Everybody's watching and everybody cares," Kevin reports.

"Damn, I hate to say it, but you're kinda right. I'm sitting here thinking about how future college athletes have televised signing days when they're in high school. It's really a big deal for the nation, but there's no nationally celebrated day when students who have straight A's decide what college they're going to. It's clear what's more important to the masses," Kennedy voices.

"Yo, when you mention academics not being important when compared to sports, it's true. Peep this, if I want to go to college as just a student I have to have a high SAT score, have participated in extracurricular activities, and have the grades to match, but it's not the same for athletes entering college. The requirements for them to get into college are much more relaxed than they are for non-athletes. That paints a pretty clear picture for me as to which one is seen as being more important," I utter.

"Exactly, now you see what I'm talking about. We even get to miss classes because we have to travel to go to away games sometimes. If academics were superior to sports, there's no way they would allow thousands of students across the country to miss valuable seat time in class. Again, sports win over academics. I'm just saying that once I noticed that, I stopped going hard for academics and went three times as hard in sports," Kevin tells us frankly.

"Son, it's crazy that it's like that, but keeping it one hundred, that's the way it is. You really don't get much shine for being smart and getting good grades. I remember last year when Quan got recognized by the news for being the student athlete of the month. The real deal is that he got recognized for being an athlete and the student had nothing to do with it. I say that because my sister has gotten straight A's since we started high school and has never been on television for it, so that clearly says to me that being an athlete is special," I orate.

Kennedy words, "The most they do for us is put our names on a sheet of paper and post them in the hallway. That's not a celebration; that's a joke."

"Bruh, with all that being said I'm still working with my sister. You gotta get it how you live. We all still have choices to make, so good luck with that," I say.

Laughingly, Kevin asks, "We'll can I at least look at your notes?"

I hesitate for a moment before I answer his question. I compare my notes to my sister's notes to see if she has anything that I don't and vice versa. Our notes pretty much contain the same information, so I let Kevin get the notes. He walks off to find a partner. Kennedy and I start working on our assignment. This sort of thing is why it's difficult to focus on certain things. Do you stick with something like academics that gets little to no attention or do you focus on sports that garner all the attention?

REFLECTION

I've seen countless students pour all of their attention, effort, and energy into playing sports. Children will really become completely absorbed in sports and not give much else any attention. Why is this happening? The reason is quite simple. The reason students who are athletes place more of their hard work into sports is because society cares more about sports than academics. Students are very impressionable and follow societal norms at a high rate even though they feel they're all extremely different from the person sitting next to them.

The fact that society cares more about sports than academics is shown on a daily basis. This is apparent in the fact that athletes are able to miss valuable seat time in the classroom in order to play sports. If sports are only a game and don't trump academics, there would never be a situation where students would miss being proctored to go play a game. The only other situation where students can be absent from class and not be penalized is if there's a health issue. Allowing students to miss time in school to go play sports means sports are just as important as health issues and doctor's appointments.

Another truth that portrays sports as being more important than academics is dealing with acceptable standards. What do I mean by acceptable standards? I'm speaking to what is considered to be acceptable for athletes is different for students who aren't athletes. For example, an athlete who wants to attend a college or university doesn't have to have the same scores as a student who just plans to focus on schoolwork. A person who's being recruited by a college for sports doesn't have to have grades nearly as high as the student who isn't going to play sports. Also, the potential athlete isn't required to have the same well-rounded portfolio as a regular student. Additionally, athletes don't even need to have the same SAT score as non-athletes in order to gain acceptance to the university. The bar is lowered for athletes and clearly paints a picture that sports are more important.

My tenure as a high school English teacher has also shown me that many parents care more about sports than academics. I taught many students who were athletes over the years. The stark reality is that many of those parents would constantly call coaches to discuss their child's athletic situation, but would not return my calls or emails pertaining to their child's poor academic performance. It was not uncommon for parents and students to miss open house nights because of games or practice. This vividly shows that society worships sports and not academics.

Think about the way sports are celebrated for a moment. People fill arenas, stadiums, and many other venues that sports are facilitated in and go crazy over them. These people are called sports fans. The word fans is short for fanatics. A fanatic is someone who is consumed with a crazed and irrational passion for something. This is exactly how people treat sports. I've never heard the term education fans and that's because society isn't overly obsessed about education. Furthermore, athletes who win championships are celebrated publicly. Their pictures are in newspapers, they visit the White House or State House just depending on what level of sports they're playing, and they may even get to meet the President of the United States or the governor of their state.

Thousands of students make the honor roll every marking period and never receive the celebration that athletes receive. They're lucky to have their name typed on a sheet of paper that gets hung in the hallway only to be knocked off the wall and stepped on by students. Athletes have pep rallies that interrupt class time, but students who make the honor roll are not celebrated in the same fashion, if at all. There are parades for athletes when they win championships and universities even cancel classes to ensure that their students will be free to support the teams. How is it permissible to not attend class in order to attend a sports celebration if sports aren't favored more than academics? It makes perfect sense that many students don't invest a tremendous amount of effort into school because they won't be celebrated for it anyway.

How can we help fix the situation? Society needs to pay the same amount of attention to students who are solely students as they do to students who are athletes. This may increase grades because students will see that they'll be praised for things other than sports. Also, it may result in an athlete caring more about his or her grades because they'll be praised for that too. Lowering expectations for athletes make it seem like athletics are more important than academics and it also makes it appear that athletes are mentally inferior to their counterparts. It has to be one or the other. There should be pep rallies in school where students who made the honor roll are recognized with the same vigor as the athletic pep rallies. There should even be an academic college signing day just as they do for athletes. How can they be called student-athletes when clearly athletics come first and are more revered? Maybe they should be called athlete-students or simply athletes because that seems to be more fitting.

CHAPTER 7
Christopher's Perspective

The bell rings to dismiss us from school today. The day breezed by and there wasn't any conflict. Gladly, all the talk about the fight I had with Mark died down toward the end of the day. Besides that, I saw Mark in the hallway after eighth period and he didn't say a word to me. Shockingly, when we made eye contact, he didn't stare at me for a longer than normal time nor did he give me a dirty look. According to what people were saying all day, Mark didn't even mention me. When people mentioned me to him, he downplayed everything and stated that our situation was squashed once we finished fighting.

I gather my belongings and exit the classroom. I chat with a couple of classmates as we walk down the hall. Omar, a member of the basketball team, is dribbling a basketball down the hallway and comes up to me. He tries to cross me over, but I knew that's what he was going to do, so I stick my hand out and steal the ball from him. Omar's shocked that I stole the ball from him because I'm not known for playing basketball. I'm known for being a goodie-two-shoe and that's fine with me. After I steal the rock from Omar, one of his teammates starts roasting him.

Several other people in the hallway who saw me take the ball away from Omar are clowning him too. Omar is embarrassed because he's the star of the basketball team. Even though basketball is a team sport, Omar is credited with singlehandedly winning the state championship for our school last year. He averaged better than twenty-five points a game and even hit the game winning shot in the state championship game. Omar doesn't take me stealing the ball from him lightly. He can't allow me to walk away without redeeming himself. It would hurt his pride too much.

For this reason, Omar tells me to give him the ball back, so he can cross me over this time. He claims that the basketball slipped out of his hand and that's the only reason I was able to take the rock from him. Everyone who was watching knows that's not the truth and they let Omar know it. I don't care one way or the other and consider it to be pretty meaningless in the scheme of things. Since it's all in good sport, I decide to play along with Omar. No matter what happens, I can't lose. If I don't steal the ball again, it doesn't matter because I already stole it once and I'm not a basketball player, so nobody's going to roast me if the star basketball player crosses me over. On the other hand, Omar has everything to lose because of his prestige. If I steal the ball again, they're going to ride him for the rest of the day. There's no way they'll let him live down getting his pockets picked by me because I'm a no one on the basketball scene.

"Let me get the ball back, so I can break ya damn ankles Chris. You're gonna need reconstructive surgery on them bitches after I break them. Maybe the doctor will give you some shatter proof bones," Omar states.

I can only laugh at the ridiculousness of his comments. I'm not the only one laughing either. He has several people who are watching in stitches too. I throw him the ball back and he starts dribbling. The crowd is making all sorts of sounds. One guy screams out that he's not going to catch me when I fall to the floor. I don't pay that remark any attention because I know that I'm not going to fall. Omar's pretty damn good, but he's not quick enough to make me lose my balance and fall. Besides, I've never been made to fall on the basketball court.

As he dribbles faster, he entices me to play more defense. The thud of the basketball can be heard from far away and sounds like thunder. I get hyped up by the sound of the ball bouncing and get in a defensive stance. Many people have their phones out and are broadcasting to social media. Omar dribbles between his legs two times back to back with lightning speed. I assume he's going to dribble between his legs one more time, so I reach for it, but Omar doesn't. Instead, he dribbles around his back and takes a step back. The crowd releases a loud scream and laughs at me.

"Don't reach!" Omar orders. "Next time that's gonna be your ankles and you'll be on your ass. I'm trying to tell you I'm nice bruh."

"Man, keep dribbling and stop talking. You not getting past me and you damn sure ain't gonna break my ankles. I promise you that," I reply.

Omar answers, "Aight, but don't be mad when ya ass need us to carry you home. I warned you."

Omar starts doing all sorts of maneuvers with the basketball. His handles are nothing short of amazing. He really has control of the ball mixed in with a tremendous amount of speed. I'm trying to see if I can time his dribbles just right and lunge for the ball. If I'm on point with my lunge for the ball, I'll have another clean steal. However, if I'm not on point, I'll miss the ball and probably fall as Omar predicted. The good thing for me is that I'm playing with house money, so I can't lose. I'll wait two more dribbles and then I'm going for it.

The next dribble goes in front of him and the second dribble goes behind his back. I feel that he just made a big mistake. The ball is most vulnerable behind his back because he doesn't have control of it and I know where it's going to land. The only problem is that he knows where it's going too. It's just a matter of who will get to the ball first. I gamble and reach for the rock as it's going to the other side of his body. Omar reaches for it at the same time as I do and tries to quickly dribble it to the other side of his body. Fortunately, I was able to get the tip of my finger on the ball and poke it away from him.

I retrieve the ball and the students in the hallway watching go bananas. They're screaming and laughing at Omar. Everybody's surprised that I stole the rock from Omar because I'm not exactly known for playing basketball, but Omar is. I'm not the best, but I'm no slouch either. I can definitely hold my own. Omar is livid and embarrassed and wants revenge.

"You got that shit off Chris," says Omar. "I'm bout to get mine back."

"You can't see me. I told you that my defense is crazy yo. You wasn't listening when I warned you," I reply.

"Whatever… dribble the ball and stop talking. You're running ya mouth cause you know that I'm about to run ya pockets," Omar assures arrogantly.

I don't respond because it's unnecessary.

Instead of talking about it, I decide to be about it. I dribble the ball three hard times in my left hand and then I cross over to my right hand. Omar reaches for the ball, but misses because he isn't as quick as me. The students in the hallway all have their phones out and are laughing at him. Omar gets in his defensive stance and slaps the floor with both hands. I'm ready to give him the business and then it all comes to an end.

Apparently, we're making too much noise in the hallway because the school administration has infiltrated the hallway. We all take off running in the opposite direction from which they are coming. We are scattering like roaches when the lights come on. Nobody gets caught and we all run to the exterior of the building. We figure that with all the noise we were making and the large crowd that they thought it was a riot or something. Nope, no riots here. We're just a bunch of high school kids having fun.

Many of us meet at the corner store on Bigelow and Elizabeth Ave. We reenact how we fled the scene of the basketball match in the hallway. A bunch of dudes recorded our mass exodus from the hallway. You know they've posted it on every social media forum possible. Everyone's chiming in on how lit we were while running down the hallway and clearing flights of stairs in a single bound. It was fun, but it's not like we had hit the lottery or anything. Many of the people responding to the videos claim they wish they were there. I'm not surprised because my entire generation always wishes they're involved in something even when it's not that serious. Unfortunately, most of my generation is concerned with things that aren't fruitful, but are enamored by time wasters.

Omar strolls over to the corner where we're all gathered and starts talking trash. He tells me that I was only able to get the best of him because we were in a cramped up hallway. He claims that if we were on an actual basketball court there would be a totally different outcome. I go back and forth with him just for kicks. The truth is that he might be right. I've seen him play several times and he always crosses people over.

"Yo, meet me at Weequaic Park. We can ball up over there and I'm gonna shit on you. Dead ass!" Omar words confidently.

I respond, "I gotta hit da crib first, but I'm down to go. It just depends on what time."

"Nah, you don't gotta go home. You're just scared as fuck cause you know that I'm bout dat action. Don't bitch up. Let's go now," Omar lectures.

"I hear what you're saying, but I definitely gotta hit the crib first, but I'll meet you over there at like five, five-thirty. I'm serious. On everything," I tell.

Omar is appeased by my suggestion of being at the park between five and five-thirty. Many of the other guys who are out here agree to meet at the park around that time. We plan to run some fulls and see who crosses who over and who breaks whose ankles. I'm not worried at all. I look up the block and catch a glimpse of my sister walking toward the house, so I leave the fellas on the corner and walk toward my sister.

As I'm walking to meet Kennedy, Omar shouts out, "What's good with ya sister bruh?"

I look back with a mean mug and state, "Don't play."

All of the remaining guys on the corner just laugh. Omar doesn't say anything else and neither do I. I catch up to Kennedy and we walk home. She tells me that she saw mad videos posted from the hallway. Kennedy also fills me in on parts of her day that she didn't get to tell me about earlier. When we arrive at the house, we do our homework and clean up what needs to be cleaned. The entire time that I'm home, my phone never stops buzzing from people talking about going to the park.

Five o'clock rolls around, so my sister and I start walking to Weequaic Park. We walk past the Caramel Towers and make it to the park. We head straight to the basketball court when we enter the park. I see Omar and several of our classmates sitting and standing on the outskirts of the basketball court. Unfortunately, there are people running full court basketball games, so we'll have to wait until they're done. The line for who has the next game is extremely long because there is what looks like a family reunion going on. Omar spots me and heads over to me.

"What's good bruh?" he asks as he daps me up.

"Ain't shit! I was ready to show you what's good, but it don't look like we ever gonna be able to get on the damn court," I announce.

Omar replies, "I don't know about you showing me what's up, but I do know about how I was gonna embarrass you. You know this is home court for me… I'm undefeated, but you're right, we're never gonna get on the court. It's pretty much over. They're gonna have the court on lock all day, bruh."

"Whatever man! I was ready to get it popping. It's definitely a wrap for us getting on the court unless we stay out here until midnight or something. I was just saying it looks like they're having a family reunion or something. It's crazy cause it's a damn weekday," I recite.

Kennedy states, "Well, I know I'm not staying out here that late. A girl needs her beauty sleep. Dead ass."

Omar chimes in, "Facts though. I'm about to skate soon. It does look like a family reunion, but it's really a coming home party for Derek. He just came home today, so his peeps threw him a coming home party."

"Word. That is Derek over there. Damn, I haven't seen him in years. Son, I know he did like five years at least," I say.

"True, he did like four and some change in Northern State. It does seem like forever ago. I remember when they locked him up cause I was with his brother when the police ran down and locked him up," Omar voices.

"Are you talking about Derek's brother, Damon?"

"Yeah, his brother Damon. I was with Damon when they locked Derek up back in the day. Yo, it was crazy as hell! I just froze up and couldn't believe it was going down right in front of me," Omar comments.

"What's up with Damon anyway? I haven't seen him since he graduated last year," Kennedy remarks.

"I heard that he went to live with some family down south. He really wanted to get out the hood, so he dipped. He chilling though," Omar tells.

I speak, "Yo, on some other shit… It's crazy that Damon graduated last year and he didn't even have a small cookout or anything to celebrate his accomplishment. Son, he was on Chancellor Ave. the night he graduated doing nothing."

"Wow! That is crazy! But that's how it is though. I ain't saying it's right, but it's real as hell though," Kennedy comments.

"Facts… Dead ass… Facts," Omar says.

"Word. Yo, since we not getting on the court today, we gonna bounce," I voice.

Omar and I dap each other up and begin to part ways. Omar explains that he's adamant about us getting a game sometime in the near future. I assure him that it'll happen sooner than later. He accepts the confirmation on the postponed game and walks off. Kennedy and I speak to some of our other classmates for a few minutes and then we walk back to the house. I know it killed Omar for us not to play today. He wanted his revenge badly and has to wait to get it. I'm cool with it because I'll hold it over his head until we have a chance to play for real. Kennedy and I make it back to the house and relax for the night. I fall asleep while watching television on the couch.

REFLECTION

I've seen it happen too many times to count when a person is going to jail or coming home from jail and the hood makes a big deal about it. A person can commit crime after crime and still be celebrated. A dude can commit the most egregious offense against his own people and still get a going away party. We can't reward people with parties and gifts for going to jail. We have to send a message that we don't support illegal activities especially in our own neighborhoods.

Also, we must be sure to reward our youth and other community members when they do the right things. We should throw parties for kids when they make the honor roll or when they do things that uplift one another. If we celebrate their accomplishments, more youth will jump on the bandwagon and start doing more positive things. Let's be honest and admit that most people like attention. In the majority of situations, kids want the attention to be for doing good things that make people proud. Unfortunately, things that are positive are often not highly celebrated unless it involves sports.

If kids don't get celebrated for doing positive acts, they will think that people don't care about them. It's likely that when kids see people who are known criminals getting attention, they'll figure that being a criminal isn't so bad. Behaving in this fashion may make a young person who's craving attention begin a life of crime. He or she may feel like the attention they receive for getting in trouble is better than gaining no attention at all. Celebrating people for the wrong reasons can have an adverse influence on society.

When society gives props to its community members for being a nuisance, it shows what's valued by the group and can be discouraging to people looking in. I've seen a family where one of the kids did everything she was supposed to do. She graduated high school and went to college as society favors. In the same household, her sibling went a different route. He chose a life of crime and was arrested several times. The treatment of the two different routes is where the problem is. The kid who went to college got little to no help from family members while the brother who went to jail was given all the help in the world. He was bailed out of jail numerous times and given thousands of dollars for numerous lawyers. Additionally, while he served his jail terms, he was given a monthly stipend.

One can only imagine how that made the daughter of the family feel. Things like this happen far too many times, but really they should be non-existent. People who do the right thing should be rewarded and people who don't do what's right should be penalized. It shouldn't be the other way around. If we send a crystal-clear message to our youth that we only support positivity and things that uplift one another, then and only then will we be able to steer our youth away from criminal activity.

CHAPTER 8
Christopher's Perspective

Morning arrives and I'm still on the couch with my clothes on from yesterday's basketball game that never happened. I was beat and didn't even know it. What time is it? I find my phone stuffed between the couch cushions and hit the button for the screen to light up, but it doesn't. Damn, my battery is dead. Kennedy walks out of her room as I'm waking up.

"Oh, I didn't know you were up. I was just about to wake you up, so you can get ready for school," Kennedy states.

"Yeah, I'm up. Yo, I didn't even know I was sleep. I was just sitting out here chilling and then it was morning. I don't even know how I got this blanket on me. I know I didn't get up and get it," I speak.

"I can't believe you're serious right now. I

really can't, but you were sleeping hard as hell last night. I tried to wake you up, but you wouldn't budge even though you told me twice that you were gonna get up," Kennedy reports.

I don't take her seriously because I just wasn't that tired. There's no way she attempted to wake me up once and I didn't respond. For her to say she tried to wake me up twice is just preposterous. Kennedy tells me that she's the one who put the blanket on me because I was curled up on the couch with my arms in my sleeves as if I were cold. She then proceeds to pull out her phone and show me a video that she posted to SnapChat of her attempting to wake me up. I'm astonished that I didn't wake up because I'm normally a light sleeper. My sister also shows me the second video she posted on SnapChat of her trying to wake me up a second time. I crack up laughing at my reluctance to get off the couch. Well, at least I slept well.

"Thanks, for the blanket," I say.

"Don't thank me now, Mr. I didn't try to wake you up," Kennedy shoots back jokingly.

I reply, "My bad. I was out like a light. On everything, I think somebody drugged me. That's the only logical explanation for me passing out like that."

"Umm, ain't nobody drug ya ass. Don't nobody want you!" Kennedy tells me. "What you need to do is get up and get ready for school. Hurry up cause I wanna stop by the store first."

I do as my sister requests and jump up off the couch. I hit the shower and get dressed in no time. We leave the house and head over to the corner store. Poppy has the best breakfast sandwiches and Kennedy wants to get one before school. I'm not hungry, so I don't get a sandwich. Instead, I just grab a bag of chips to eat during the school day if I get hungry before lunch. While we're in the store, we hear several cop car sirens blaring. When we walk out the store to head to school and see the cop cars have stopped on our block. They are four houses down from our house on Milford Ave.

My sister and I stop on the corner to get a good vantage point of what the cops are doing. We still have some time before school starts, so we can see what's going on without being late to school. The cops are out of their cars and on the porch about to enter the house when we hear the cops yelling out. Apparently, whoever they're chasing is climbing out the back window of the house. Several cops proceed through the front door, while others run along the side of the house to gain access to the backyard.

We can't see what's going on in the backyard from where we are, so we decide to continue to school. All we know is that the police have the house surrounded and it's not likely that whoever they're looking for is going to get away. As soon as we look away from the scene with the cops, we hear a man scream loudly. We immediately turn around and see the cops escorting a man from the backyard in handcuffs.

"Get the fuck off me! You pigs are always fucking with people. Let me go! I ain't do shit," the handcuffed man screams out angrily.

One cop speaks, "You have the right to remain silent. Anything you say…"

The guy in cuffs blurts out, "Fuck you and those rights! Let me go! These cuffs are too tight. They are cutting my fucking wrists!"

The dude is clearly disgruntled about the entire situation. He's so mad that we begin to think that maybe he is innocent. I know how I act when someone blames me for something I didn't do and he's acting exactly like that. Unfortunately, he makes a move that he's sure to regret. He tries to pull away from the cops and inadvertently or purposely hits one officer in the face with his shoulder.

Kennedy asks rhetorically, "Now, why did he do that?"

"I think he wants to get his ass beat. That's all I can think of because there are too many officers around him for him to think that he was gonna break free and get away," I answer while shaking my head.

"Facts Chris, and don't forget the handcuffs. He's wilding for no reason at all. Oh snap! That's Jermaine they have in cuffs! Look at his face," Kennedy speaks.

"Oh shit! That is Jermaine. They finally

caught up to him. Damn, that's crazy as hell that he was hiding right on our block and we didn't even know it," I respond.

Kennedy speaks, "That's what I was thinking. Well, he did avoid being caught for the last couple of months, so I guess that's good. He was right down the street from us and we never even saw him."

"Word. He must have only been out of the house at night because otherwise we would have seen him. There's no way we wouldn't have seen him. Wonder if they had a reward out for him. That would've been lit if we coulda got some bread for turning him in," I convey.

"Boy bye! You know you wouldn't have turned him in for no reward money. The only way you woulda snitched is if we were gonna be in trouble if you didn't tell," Kennedy shoots back.

I don't deny what she said because it's true. I would never just volunteer information that would send someone to jail. I know it's not right, but it's the code of the streets. Everyone knows that snitches get stitches and I don't want any problems. The entire hood would turn their backs on you if they knew you reported someone to the police. Jermaine is a drug dealer and has been on the run ever since the beginning of the summer. At the start of the summer, many of the drug dealers in the area were arrested as part of the normal summer sweep of criminals. Secret indictments as they are called, always remove many drug dealers from the streets. We heard they went to Jermaine's crib on Renner Avenue and spin kicked the door, but he wasn't there. He's been on the run ever since. They finally nabbed him.

The cop who got hit in the jaw when Jermaine pulled away isn't taking the blow lightly. He and the other officers slam Jermaine to the ground and give him a taste of his own medicine. They are really beating him down. Jermaine is wailing in pain. I knew it was a bad choice when he pulled away from the cop. I wonder if he feels the same way too. We don't want to stop watching, but we have to leave now if we want to make it to school before the late bell rings. We walk to school and converse about what we've just witnessed.

"Damn, I'm low-key kinda mad that they caught Jermaine. I know he was hustling, but he was alright with me. He was a good dude for the most part," I state.

"Right, that's facts bruh! He always was one hundred with me. Like, he was a better person to me than people who weren't selling drugs. I remember one day when it was hot as hell outside, Jermaine bought all of us soda from the corner store," Kennedy narrates.

"Son, I remember when he bought my boy a pair of sneakers because his sneakers were too small and had holes in them. You gotta respect a dude like that. Shit, even the counselors at the school weren't doing that," I vocalize.

"I know right. Ain't nobody at the school spending their own money to help us out. Jermaine was holding us down. Bruh, if you think about it, nothing has changed since they locked all of those people up at the beginning of the summer," Kennedy remarks.

"Yo, I was about to say the same thing. Dead ass! They arrested all of those people in that drug operation, but the drug selling never stopped. It's like what they did was pointless. People were still getting high and overdosing. Not to mention that people have still been getting killed over drug territory," I comment.

"I don't know what to think about what's going on out here, but it sure seems fishy to say the least," Kennedy words.

"You ain't never lied," I say.

We make it inside the school and get to homeroom right before the bell rings. We tell our classmates what we saw this morning and they are also upset that Jermaine got caught. Many of them take to social media and make posts to free Jermaine. Somebody even suggests starting a GoFundMe account for Jermaine. They can do that if they want, but I know who won't be contributing a dime to his fund and that's me. I don't have much money to begin with and I definitely don't have cash to give away.

REFLECTION

This is a situation that occurs frequently in the African American community. Drug dealers are often glorified in their communities. The reason why this is such an egregious occurrence is because these people are celebrated for actively breaking the law. Now, I understand that many drug dealers often give to the people in the communities in which they live, but that should not overshadow what harm they are doing to their neighborhoods. We can't sweep the detriments they provide to their neighborhoods under the rug.

Let's be honest; drugs have no place in these neighborhoods because they're harmful. Drugs are harmful because of the negative impacts they have on the people who use them. Basically, drug dealers are poisoning their own communities. Pushing illegal substances is also hurting the drug dealers. They are being harmed because they are being sentenced to long jail terms once they're caught. Not only are they being arrested, they are also being murdered by other individuals who are their opposition in the drug game. Everyone loses in this situation because families are adversely impacted by the illegal drug business. Families are broken up because family members are in jail, dead, or strung out on drugs.

Unfortunately, many citizens in poor

neighborhoods don't have many opportunities to grow financially. In fact, they often don't have any viable options to grow financially, so they turn to illegal activities. In many cases, they're in dire situations and don't have proper leadership, so they get sucked into the streets. Sadly, once they're sucked into the streets, many are never able to get out.

Many people in poor neighborhoods feel like their needs are being ignored by the government. It is the duty of the government to protect its citizens, but that's not happening in poor communities. It's almost like crime is allowed to rise in certain neighborhoods like Newark, but in upscale areas, crime is thwarted at its inception. Crime's not allowed to spread like a wildfire in areas where white people dominate. Why is that the case?

Again, people in poor neighborhoods lose hope because it doesn't seem like help is ever going to come. The government initiated a War on Drugs, but it doesn't seem like that's the case. It really looks like the government created a war on black people. That's how many people feel and it's for good reason. If the war was really on drugs, it wouldn't have resulted in thousands of jail sentences for African Americans.

We all know that white America uses drugs at the same rate as black people, but somehow white people aren't penalized as frequently or as long as blacks. Additionally, it isn't black people who are transporting drugs from other continents and bringing them to their location. Also, it's very hard to believe that black people make up a minority of the population in America, but the prison population is mostly comprised of black people. Magically, our communities are riddled with drugs, but white neighborhoods are not. I guess black neighborhoods attract drugs somehow. How are drugs getting from other continents and making their way to the demographic that has the least amount of resources? Additionally, African Americans make up the vast majority of the prison population. These are questions that people are asking, but aren't getting any answers.

It appears that black people are being setup to be held back. Let's examine why people feel the way they do by looking at the supposed war on drugs. The first thing I ask is how do you solve a problem that exists? First, you have to recognize that a problem exists. Secondly, you have to find the source of the problem and then seek ways to remove the problem. Lastly, you have to implement the strategies to expunge the problem completely or have a goal to reduce the problem incrementally over a stated time period. Has this happened with the war on drugs in the black community? No, the only thing that happened was that black people started getting jailed at an extremely high rate and companies benefitted from their arrests.

The government's efforts did not work for what the stated goal was supposed to be. The street level black people were jailed at a tremendously high rate and it caused the prison population of blacks to swell. If that wasn't the goal, the government would have switched their approach to end the problem. Jailing people in drug raids was not the answer to solving a huge epidemic.

The first thing that should have been done was to hit the source of the illegal drug selling in those neighborhoods. The source of the problem was the effects of poverty, such as low income, low education, and little to no hope. Therefore, the government should have created an onslaught of programs that addressed those issues. Then, the best move would have been to go after the source of the drugs. If there's no supply of drugs, people can't abuse them. Everyone knows that when you take a street level drug dealer off the streets he or she is replaced with another drug dealer by the time the cops pull off the block, so it doesn't make sense to keep locking up low level drug dealers and giving them extremely long prison terms.

When truly attempting to eradicate a problem, you have to monitor and adjust what strategies you have installed. If they aren't working, the best move is to switch them up and try another approach. Now, if you're happy with your results, you keep running the same game plan as when you initially started. Another way to expunge the drug epidemic would be to get rid of the demand for it. That would require extensive drug rehab programs for the people who are abusing drugs. From what I've seen, the government would use the drug addicts to help catch the people who were selling the drugs, but wouldn't regularly place the drug addicts in treatment facilities. Furthermore, the addicts would be offered a free pass for possessing the drugs if they were willing to help the cops lock up the person who sold them the drugs. Is the goal to simply arrest drug pushers who will be quickly replaced or to heal the sick? It really looks like the goal is to lock up the black people who sell drugs, but never get rid of the causes of why drugs are sold and used. That's why black people feel the "War on Drugs" was a war against them.

I'll use a short story to flush out my point. Imagine that I own a business that sells hamburgers. The problem is that a lot of people love my hamburgers, but my hamburgers make the people who eat them sick. Coincidentally, my hamburger stores are predominantly located in poor black areas. Years later, the CDC decides that my hamburger stores are causing too many issues in the communities they are in. The CDC decides that they have to step in to solve the problem. Their solution to the problem is to arrest my employees. I respond by hiring more employees to run my hamburger stores. Again, the CDC arrests my new employees. For years, the CDC continues locking my employees up. During this time, I receive new customers as well as repeat customers. My hamburger store is flourishing like never before. Unfortunately, thousands of my customers have died and my employees' families are devastated.

Is the CDC's plan working? Of course, the plan isn't working. If the plan was to keep people from eating my hamburgers, the CDC failed miserably. If they wanted to stop people from eating my hamburgers, they would have diminished my hamburger source and they would have treated my customers. Removing my employees was pointless because there are always people who are willing to work. If there are no burgers to be sold, there's no business. No product, no employees, and no customers equals problem solved. This should be the approach with getting rid of drugs on our streets. If the drug dealers don't have any customers or a supply, they will be out of business.

CHAPTER 9
Christopher's Perspective

It's another great Friday and I can't wait for this school day to be over. It's not great because something magical is going on, but it's great because it's Friday and the weekend is almost upon us! I don't have any major plans even though my sister and I are going to the football game tonight. We're playing Central High School tonight and everybody's supposed to be going. The bell to end homeroom is ringing, so we exit the class.

I walk into the hallway and everyone's talking about the football game tonight. The starting quarterback for our team is in the hallway and is souped up about tonight's game. He's telling everyone that we're going to win. He's even guaranteeing a blowout victory. I'm not surprised that he's talking so assuredly because he's definitely nice at what he does. In fact, he's already been offered full scholarships to several different schools. He hasn't accepted any of the offers yet, but rumor has it that he's going to go to NC State.

While we're all in the hallway chatting, Omar walks up. He joins in the conversation about tonight's game. Several of us talk about riding to the game together. Central has some very pretty females who go there and all of the fellas are planning to holler at a few of them. Omar even suggests that we go to Weequaic Park to get in the basketball game that we were unable to get in the other day. I know he's never going to let it go, so I agree to meet him at the park today.

"Yo, I'm down to ball up, but it has to be right after school this time. That way we can play and still have time to shower up and make it to the game on time," I speak.

Omar states, "That's what's up! We'll run like two fulls and then bounce. If we leave as soon as school ends, we'll have plenty of time to rock out."

"Facts! I'll head to the park as soon as the bell rings," I reply.

Omar also says that he'll be heading to the park when the bell rings. We solicit the attendance of other classmates as well. They also agree to meet us over there. Some of the guys who agree to come to the park are on the basketball team and others are just pretty good street ball players. Additionally, one of the girls on the girl's team says that she's coming to play too. The bell alerting us that we have one minute to get to class rings, so I depart from the group and go to class.

Before I know it, lunch time is here. I hit the cafeteria as soon as the bell sounds. When I get to the cafeteria, my phone chimes. I look at my phone and see that Omar has hit me up again. I open the message and it's a video of Steph Curry getting crossed over by Kyrie Irving in the NBA Finals. I'm dying laughing because his caption says that it's going to be me getting crossed over like that. He even managed to superimpose my face over Steph Curry's face. I'm cracking up laughing while watching the video. This guy won't stop with the videos. Earlier he sent me a video of Allen Iverson breaking several NBA players' ankles back in the day and also claimed that I'll be receiving broken ankles today.

I haven't responded to any of the videos even though they're hilarious. Instead, I'll save all of my trash talking for once we get on the court. All of the stuff he's sending is light-hearted and in the fun of the sport. I go grab my lunch and sit down to eat. I don't see Kennedy, so I shoot her a text to see where she is. She's normally in here by now. Moments later, my phone chimes again. I think it's Kennedy, but it's not. Omar sent me another video clip.

Before I have a chance to open his message, Kennedy texts me back. She's on her way to the cafeteria now and tells me to save her a seat. I eat my lunch and listen to music. After a few minutes, Kennedy joins me. Kennedy has a smug look on her face, so I take my headphones off to investigate why she has that look on her face.

"I already know something's wrong, so you might as well spit it to me. Ya face is telling me that something is bothering you," I voice.

"Hell yeah, something's bothering me. I guess you haven't seen the video that you're in because if you did, you'd be mad like I am," Kennedy replies.

"Damn, I didn't think that you'd be mad over that video. I thought that joint was funny as hell to be honest. I was cracking up the whole time I was watching it. On everything, I couldn't wait to show you. I thought you were gonna think it was funny too," I state.

"No, I didn't think it was funny at all. I really thought it was tasteless and will only cause more trouble going forward," Kennedy offers.

"Sis, I don't see how you think that video is gonna cause trouble. It was meant to be funny. Omar isn't sweating that video. He likes it too," I word.

"Omar doesn't have anything to do with this. Bruh, if you don't think another video of you beating up Mark isn't a problem, you're retarded," Kennedy tells.

"Wait, I thought you were talking about the video of Omar crossing me over with our faces superimposed over Steph Curry and Kyrie Irving. I haven't seen a new fight video. Here we go with the bullshit," I vocalize.

"Oh, now I see why you were taking it so lightly. I thought you were losing your mind. Yeah, there's another video out there with your face superimposed over Roy Jones Jr. and then Mark's face is superimposed over another fighter's face. They have you beating Mark senseless. It's so bad. I think if he sees it, he's going to be livid," Kennedy reports.

"Damn, that's crazy! I wanna see that joint," I say.

"I got it right here. Tosha sent it to me," Kennedy replies.

My sister pulls the video up and it's pretty bad. They have me pummeling a guy with Mark's face inside of a professional boxing ring. I can clearly tell that it's one of Roy Jones Jr.'s early fights. The fight is totally one sided in my favor. I cringe each time a blow is landed on the guy because I know how Mark will feel if he sees it. He's going to be infuriated all over again. I wish I could scrub this video from the internet completely, but I know I can't. It kills me how people always keep situations going. I hope this doesn't blow up again.

As I'm talking to my sister about the video, my phone chimes alerting me to a message. I open the message and see the video of the superimposed fight. I guess since it finally reached me that it must be in heavy rotation. Well, there's nothing I can do about it at this point, so I calm down and enjoy lunch with my sister. About ten minutes later, lunch ends and we head to class. As we walk to class, many people report seeing the video. As always, I downplay its impact and go to class.

The rest of the school day is uneventful. Surprisingly, it even flew past. The bell to release us from school is moments away from ringing, so we're all standing at the door waiting to burst out of it. Everyone's still talking about the football game tonight. I'm excited about the football game, but I'm more hyped about the basketball game we're having at Weequaic Park when the day ends. The bell rings and we leave. I start receiving text messages confirming that we're still on for our scheduled basketball game.

Like all Fridays, the students depart the campus in record time. It's almost like a ghost town around here. My sister and I walk down the street to head home. While we're heading home, an all-black Charger drives past. We don't think anything about it until the same black Charger drives past again. The car slows down a little bit and the window starts to ease down. I see the face of the guy where the window is rolling down from. To my dismay, it's Mark. He begins to raise his hand out of the window as if he has a gun. My sister and I duck down behind a parked car. I don't know which way is best for us to run, but if I hear that car door open up, we're going to bolt out of here. I look up to see what Mark's doing. I can see that his hand is empty, but he has his hand out of the window configuring it as if he's pulling the trigger of a gun. While he's doing that, a car pulls up behind the car he's in and beeps the horn. The black Charger pulls off. We stand up from our hiding place and bolt home. We don't care to see that car again.

We make it to the house without seeing Mark again. I really don't have the energy or patience to deal with Mark's shenanigans. I'm really just focused on finishing school and getting out of the hood, but it seems like many others are not. I change out of the clothes I wore to school and put on my basketball gear. After that, I head over to Weequaic Park to play basketball. While I'm walking to the park, the basketball court comes into my line of sight. I see several of the homies from school. They're already warming up. I know that this is going to be some serious balling up today. I get to the court and warm up a little. I don't need much time to warm up because I'm in great shape and the walk over has me loose to a slight degree.

I dap up all of the fellas, but I don't see Omar. I know he's not ducking me now. After all of that trash talking, he has to show up. Honestly, I'm not looking forward to playing against anyone other than him. Not that playing against them won't be fun, but the main attraction for me is to go toe to toe with Omar. I decide to call Omar to make sure he's still coming. As I'm dialing his number, I see a car pull up that looks like Omar's brother's car. I pause for a second to see if Omar emerges from the car and he does. He walks over to the court and daps everyone up.

"Yo, start shooting for teams," somebody shouts.

"I'll shoot first, but no matter what happens me and Omar are not on the same team and I'm sticking him the whole game. I'm about to lock his ass down again like I did in the hallway," I vocalize.

Omar replies, "Bruh, you got that off in the hallway, but that was some luck type shit to keep it one hunnett. That shit ain't happening on the court today son. Hell nah, it ain't! We definitely sticking each other the whole game. Dead ass!"

I shoot back, "That's what it is! I'm shitting on you today. For real, for real. Yo, give me the ball, so I can shoot for teams."

A classmate of mine passes me the ball as I walk to the foul line to shoot for teams. I do my normal routine of giving myself two chest pounds with my fist before I shoot. Omar comments that I'm going to miss the shot, but I'm not worried. Besides, Omar is just trying to get in my head for the game. However, it's not going to work. I release the ball toward the basket, but unfortunately, I miss the shot.

Omar states, "I told ya ass you were gonna miss. Broke ass shot... You can't shoot!"

I throw Omar the ball and tell him to shoot, since he has so much to say. He catches the rock and steps to the foul line. He bricks the shot off the left side of the rim and I start laughing at him. He bricks the shot so hard that he has to chase down the rebound. I hope these two missed open shots aren't indicative of the types of games we're going to have today. I at least have to put up a decent effort today.

Another guy steps to the line to shoot to see who will pick the teams, but he misses too. If we all keep missing, we'll never get the game going. At this rate, it'll be time for us to get ready for the football game and we won't even have started this game. I figure out there is a better way. Since Omar and I don't want to be on the same team, it's only right that we should be the ones to pick for teams. This will surely speed up the process and help get the game started. I pitch my suggestion to the fellas and they all acquiesce. I let Omar pick first just to get things rolling. We quickly pick our teams and are set. Since Omar picked first, my team gets the ball first.

I bring the ball up the court for our team. I cross half court and approach the three-point line. Omar meets me at the three-point line to play defense, but doesn't have his hand up to properly defend my shot. I know I have caught him slipping with this subpar defense, so I seize the opportunity. I spread my fingers and flick my wrist as I shoot a jump shot from three-point land. The shot goes straight through the net without hitting anything. Omar shakes his head as the ball swishes through the net. I jet back down court to get ready to play defense. I know Omar is going to come right back at me, so I need to be ready.

As expected, Omar has the peel in his possession and is dribbling up the court. He makes it to the top of the key and his teammate comes to set a pick for him, but Omar frowns and waves him away. Clearly, Omar wants an isolation situation. He wants to take me off the dribble and doesn't want any help in scoring from anyone. I step up and Omar dribbles three times quickly between his legs and goes to pull up for the jumper from just inside the three-point line. I go to smack the ball out of his hand, but my calculation is off. Omar wasn't going for a jump shot he just wanted me to think that. Instead, he executes a flawless hesitation dribble and breezes by me and goes to the rack for an uncontested layup.

"You got a brother named Reach!" Omar screams as he runs back up the court.

Damn, he caught me reaching and I paid for it. I'll know better next time for sure. I see several people on the sideline of the basketball court laughing at me. I totally understand why they're laughing because I would be laughing too. I'm not mad or embarrassed because I know that I'm going to get mine again. I bring the ball up the court again, but this time Omar puts tighter defensive pressure on me. I guess he doesn't want me to drain another jumper in his eyes. I see my teammate moving in my direction to set a pick and I plan to use it. Once he sets the pick, I dribble in his direction and force Omar into him. Fortunately, the pick works to perfection because Omar and his partner get jammed up and can't move. I jump in the air to take the open shot, but I see my teammate rolling to the basket without a defender, so I pass him the ball and he dunks the ball with two hands. The entire park quaked from the force of his dunk.

We run back down court slapping hands and cheering. We are completely hyped now and there's no bringing us down. Omar has the ball in his hands again when he crosses half court, but doesn't hold it for long. His teammate spins off of his defender and runs to the basket. Omar sees his teammate making his way to the basket and throws him the perfect ally hoop. The rim and backboard rattle from the dunk. Both teams are lit and won't relent. Neither team is afraid of the other and we're going at it.

We continue playing with extreme intensity throughout the game. Omar is scoring on me and I'm scoring on him. It's like Jordan versus Kobe out here and all of the spectators are locked into the game as if they're playing it themselves. The game is knotted up at 10 and we're playing straight up to 11. There's no win by two today because we want to finish quickly, so we can hit the football game. Omar's team has the ball and is bringing the ball up the court. Omar is down on the block and we're battling for position. Omar's partner passes him the ball in the paint and he catches it. Omar throws a head fake, but I don't fall for it. Next, he takes two dribbles and drop steps across the lane and releases a shot. I jump to try to block his shot, but it glides just over my fingertip, rolls around the rim, and falls through the hoop. Omar's team wins the game.

Omar yells, "Game time! Next! Get these boys off the court!"

I say, "Nah, yo run it back... Run dat shit back. We got time for another one. It's only like four thirty."

A few dudes who were waiting to play in the next game are opposed to us running it back. Omar is talking mad trash about how he dusted me off and that I can't stop him. I tell the other dudes to let us run it back, but they won't give in. I go back and forth with them, but my efforts are futile, so I just fall back. I know I did my thing out there, but I still want to play. It's not happening, so I walk to the bench to sit down.

"Yo, Chris. Take my spot. I ain't staying that long anyway," Cedric says.

"Word! Good looking out bruh," I respond.

I jump up and quickly head back to the court before Cedric changes his mind. I tell everyone that I'm guarding Omar again. His team won, so they get to bring the ball up first. Omar dribbles past half court and I meet him right there. He attempts to cross over and dribble past me, but he's unsuccessful. I tip the ball away from him and run to it. I catch up to the ball, dribble it, and lay it up for an uncontested shot.

The game goes back and forth very similar to the first one. Everyone on the court is putting in work. There are no easy baskets. We all have to scrape and fight for everything. Just like the previous game, the score is tied up at ten to ten, but this time my team has the ball. There's no way that I'm not taking the shot. I dribble straight up the court to the top of the key. Omar pushes up on me. I can tell he doesn't want me to make the game winning shot, but I am. I dribble left and right and he follows me. I can't get any space, so I back up to get some room and plan where I'm taking the shot from. I'm well beyond the three-point line, so Omar doesn't follow me. Instead, he waits for me right at the line.

I dribble to the line again and fake like I'm about to pull up from the three-point line. Omar goes to block the shot, but I use his hesitation move on him and dribble past while he's in the air. Unfortunately, I don't have a clear path to the basket, so I shoot a jump shot from the foul line and it goes in. My team wins the game! Omar and I jaw back and forth for a few more minutes. It's all in good spirit. After we talk trash, we give each other props for playing well and then we depart the park, so we can get ready for the football game.

I make it home in no time and see Kennedy is almost ready. I'm glad she's not still in the bathroom doing her makeup because I'm able to beeline for the shower. Within thirty minutes of reaching the crib, I'm showered, dressed, and ready to go. I tell Kennedy about the basketball game while we wait for her homegirl to pick us up. She informs me that she saw some of the games' events live on Instagram. I'm not one bit surprised. We get to the game with no problems, but it's taking us forever to find a parking space. We end up parking on the street in front of someone's house and walking over to the game. The game is packed even more than we anticipated. It looks like the Million Man March out here. We walk around talking to friends as the game goes on.

The game itself is great! The score is tied up in the fourth quarter with five minutes to go. I decide to find a good spot to post up at, so I don't miss any of the remaining action. My sister and her friend continue roaming the football stadium. Central has the ball and is driving toward their end zone. They're moving the ball steadily and the clock is moving even faster. I can tell the Shabazz supporters are getting nervous because they aren't cheering like they were moments ago.

There are now two minutes left and the ball is on the twenty yard line. Central is in field goal range already, so even if they don't score a touchdown, they are likely to get a field goal. I'm a bit antsy myself to be honest. They run a couple of plays and pick up eight yards in total. It's now third and two with a minute and ten seconds to go. Central runs another play and picks up another first down. It's first and goal with fifty-two seconds to go.

Central runs a running play, but only nets a yard. Shabazz calls a timeout immediately with thirty-eight seconds on the clock. The time out is over before we know it and the teams are lined up again. The ball is pitched to the outside and they pick up two yards. The guy is tackled out of bounds, so the clock stops at thirty seconds even. It is now third and seven and time is almost expired. I look to their sideline and can see their kicker getting ready just in case.

The teams are lined up again and the ball is snapped. Central runs the ball and gains six yards after their star running back danced around and looked like he was going to lose yards on the play. Central calls their last time out with twelve seconds left. Their field goal unit comes on the field to prepare for the kick. Everyone's lined up and the crowd is at full attention. Shabazz's fans begin making noise in hopes to distract Central's kicker. They snap the ball and the kick is blocked! Aaron manages to throw one of Central's linemen out of the way and block the kick. Aaron recovers the ball and runs it straight to the end zone to win the game as time expires. Our entire fan base goes bananas and Aaron's teammates swarm him.

I exclaim, "That was lit as fuck!"

Everyone's sharing posts about what just happened. We all celebrate the dramatic win at the last second. I talk to some people I know for about thirty more minutes, but the police start forcing everyone to disperse. I send my sister a text to tell her to meet me at the car, so we can dip. When I arrive at the car, they're sitting inside waiting on me. I jump in the car and we bounce. We're hungry, so we hit the White Castle on Lyons Ave. We order from the drive thru, pick up our food, and head home.

We pull up to our crib and notice a tremendous amount of smoke coming from the roof. The third floor is on fire! Kennedy and I look in amazement as the fire builds. We don't know what to do other than to call 911. They inform us that the fire department has been dispatched. The people who live upstairs and downstairs from us are running out of the apartment building. The drug dealers who live in the building are carrying their personal belongings and putting them in their cars. I'm sure they're stashing their drugs in their cars too.

Just a minute later, the cops arrive. Surprisingly, two of the cops who are first to arrive at the scene are two of the dirty cops who regularly rob the drug dealers. They run over and ask if everyone's out of the building. I know that my sister and I are good, so I don't even respond. The cops ask the lady who lives upstairs the same question again. She tells him that all of her kids are out of the building. The cops come to our place regularly, so they know everyone who lives in the building.

The cop asks, "Where is little Ray?"

His mom responds horrifically, "Oh my God! He's still in his bed. I didn't wake him up!"

One of the cops runs into the house without hesitation. The mom of the child is now crying uncontrollably. She's fearing the worst. The drug dealer is even upset with himself because it's his little brother who's still in the house. My sister and I just hug each other as the top floor burns up. A minute later, the cop who ran in the building, emerges with little Ray in his arms. We can't tell if he's dead or alive. Simultaneously, the fire department pulls up. They work on the boy until the ambulance arrives. It looks like he's going to be alright. They tell us that he's going to need to be treated for smoke inhalation.

"That cop saved Ray's life. He woulda burned to death or choked to death," I voice.

Kennedy states, "Hell yeah! That's sad that

they left him to die like that. It's pitiful when ya own mother and brother don't realize that you're still in a burning house. That's fucked up!"

"Facts! That's facts though! Dead ass!" I say.

The fire department finally has the fire extinguished and is leaving. They told us that we can't go back into our apartment for the night. However, tomorrow we can go back inside. We really dodged a bullet by not being home when the fire started because we could have been seriously harmed or even killed. Additionally, we made out great because our unit didn't suffer any damage other than a little water damage to the ceiling, but our apartment is still habitable. We would have been devastated if we couldn't come back home. Unfortunately, the people who live upstairs from us aren't so lucky. Their unit received the brunt of the fire and water damage, so they can't go back into their place at all. It's a total loss according to the fire department officials. My sister and I go to her friend's house to spend the night. It looks like I'll be sleeping on someone's floor tonight. I don't like it, but it's better than being dead or burnt up from a fire.

REFLECTION

We've all seen videos of police officers killing black children and men in the streets. No matter how many times we see these atrocious acts, we never get used to them. Black people have grown over time to have a huge distrust of the police. However, the distrust that has been formed is not without validation. Life events are hard to process and can be even harder to process when things are blurred. There's no one way to look at a lot of things that happen in life. For this reason, children should be coached through traumatic situations when they occur.

As stated, black people have a distrust of the police. The problem with that is that all cops aren't dirty cops. Most of them do the job they swore to do, but get a bad reputation because of the actions of a few. Black youth have a hard time processing whether the police are good or bad because of the cops' varying behaviors. How can a child really form a clear opinion on the police when they see so many conflicting actions done by them?

In the case of Kennedy and Chris, they've experienced the police robbing drug dealers of money they made illegally. Now, they know that the duty of the cops isn't to steal drug money and put it in their pockets, but they do anyway. That act is conflicting in itself. A kid may say the cops are wrong for robbing the drug dealers, but in the same breath, a kid may say that the cops aren't so bad because they didn't arrest the drug dealers. One could argue that the cops did the drug dealers a solid by not locking them up and allowing them to stay on the streets with their families. Someone else could argue just as easily that the cops are totally wrong for their behavior. It all depends on who's telling the story.

This differing behavior is what confuses many people on whether the cops can be trusted. In some instances, the cops are heroes and in other instances they're villains. The cop who pulled Ray from the burning house is one of the same cops who periodically robs the drug dealers. Any person would have trouble processing if they should or should not trust the police under these circumstances. The boy who was rescued by the cop would most likely argue that the cop is a hero, but at the same time remember that the cop is a robber too. Talk about internal conflict.

There will always be distrust of the police if things stay the way they are. The negative feelings that black people have towards the police stem from many previous generations. There has always been inconsistent treatment of black people from the police. The scars black people received during the Civil Rights Movement have not healed. The damage from water hoses, dogs, and brutal beatings continuously plague our minds. The killings of Tamir Rice, Freddie Gray, and countless other black people, remind black people how bad situations still are.

We may never heal from those despicable events. We may never fully trust the police, but the relationship between the black community and cops can get better. We need for the police to be consistent with their treatment of us. They need to deal with black people the same way they deal with white people. Also, the patience cops have when dealing with white people needs to be extended to black people. There is a clear difference in the way the lives of blacks are valued when compared to whites. Black people seem to be expendable, while white lives are cherished. This is apparent in the fact that the rate that black people are murdered by the police is much higher than the rate they kill white people.

When black people are accosted by the police, they are treated as criminals and aren't given the benefit of the doubt. Black people are seen as threats and violent individuals. They are often targeted and pulled over at a higher rate than white people. The racial profiling has to end if relationships between blacks and the police are going to get better. Lastly, if relations are going to get better, police have to be prosecuted when they commit wrongdoings to black people. Additionally, the charges have to lead to criminal convictions. Once fair treatment, arrests, prosecution, and convictions are installed, the relationship between black people and the police will begin to become fortified.

CHAPTER 10
Christopher's Perspective

I awake to my alarm clock blaring. It's Monday morning and time to rise and shine to get ready for school. The weekend was bitter sweet for me. The sweet part was that I held my own against Omar in the basketball games on Friday and our school won the football game. The bad part was that our crib caught fire. My clothes smell like smoke, but I have no choice other than to wear them. Keeping it one hundred, it seems like getting to live another day around here in Brick City isn't so easy. People are getting killed left and right out here, so we're just blessed to see another day.

My sister and I get dressed and then eat some bacon and eggs. After we finish eating, I clean up the kitchen and we leave. We walk to the corner store and link up with some of our classmates.

We're all out there talking about what we did this weekend. Everyone's telling stories about what they did. One of the dudes even mentions that he saw our house burning down on Instagram.

"Yo, I saw y'all crib burning down on Instagram. That was wild as hell! I was hoping that y'all wasn't home. My boy told me that nobody died, so that's a good look," he states.

I respond, "Good looks on that. Me and my sister got lucky because we weren't home and our crib didn't get much damage, but the people upstairs got hit pretty hard."

We continue with telling stories about what happened this weekend. I notice that it's almost time for the school bell to ring, so Kennedy and I continue our walk to school. The crowd of people starts walking toward the school with us. I hear a few of the people behind us mumbling something and then everybody starts laughing. I don't pay it any attention until I hear my name come from one of them.

I turn around and ask, "One of you guys said my name?"

"Nah, ain't nobody say ya name. We just talking about how hot it is out here," one of them answers.

When he says that, they all start laughing again. I don't think it being hot outside is really funny, so I figure they must have an inside joke going on. Since I heard my name, I know it's about me, but I'm not going to trip on them. I just want to make it to school on time.

"Damn, I have the craziest craving for some barbecue food. I just want some barbecue ribs or something," someone from the group behind us speaks loudly.

I know he intended for me to hear him because he said it too loudly. Once again, the group of people start laughing. This time they're laughing harder than they did the first time. I'm positive that they're roasting me, but they're being lame about it because they're not addressing me to my face. Kennedy even tells me that she thinks they're clowning me on the low. I've always been pretty witty and can joke with the best of them. I might as well investigate this a little further.

I question, "Y'all trying to roast me? Y'all got jokes?"

"I'm not saying that I'm trying to roast you, but I am saying that you and Kennedy smell like you were at a cookout before you came out today," one guy says.

Once again, the group begins laughing and my suspicions are confirmed that they were cracking jokes, but I'm okay with it because I'm well equipped for this battle. I gesture to my sister that I'm about to break all of them down. She wants me to let it go, but I'm not. This is all light-hearted fun and I don't foresee it going any further than just jokes.

"Bruh, you got jokes, but ya pockets are like a

track field because everybody runs them," I joke to Travis.

All of the guys who are walking with Travis start laughing and screaming. The reason they're laughing is because they know my joke has an element of truth to it. The fact is that Travis has been robbed on more than one occasion. Two of the times he was robbed was without the perpetrators even having a gun. Everyone who knows about his bad luck feels that he's a punk because he always gives up his money without a fight. The worst of the times he was robbed was when he was stripped of his clothing.

I remember it like it was yesterday, even though it was a few years back. It was freshmen year after a football game when he got robbed. All day long, Travis was boasting about how he was the freshest person in school because he had on a brand-new True Religion Outfit. He truly was fresh from head to toe. He had on a True Religion hat, jacket, tee shirt, and jeans. He was even rocking a pair of retro Jordans that were clearly brand new. His outfit basically cost a thousand dollars.

I can't lie, everyone was talking about his fresh outfit all day long. He was posting pictures to social media and talking slick all throughout the day. To add to it all, he was even posting pictures and videos with him counting at least a thousand dollars. We were only freshmen and he was flexing like he was a grown man with a great job or a drug dealer. I thought it was lit that he had money and a nice outfit, but I also thought it was dumb of him to flaunt his belongings like that. A person can get robbed or killed anywhere, but in a city like Newark, it's very likely that someone's going to come for you if you present yourself as a target.

I feared something might happen to him, so I cautioned him about being so ostentatious. There are a lot of people out here who are living in squalor, so they won't hesitate to take what's yours. Unfortunately, Travis didn't heed my warnings and continued be flashy and reckless publicly and it caught up to him. After the football game, my sister, a few friends, and I went to White Castle on Lyons Ave. to eat. Travis showed up to White Castle with one of his friends and posted his whereabouts to Instagram. That proved to be his tragic flaw because moments later, two dudes with masks on came inside and robbed him at gunpoint. They ran his pockets and made him take off his entire outfit. We all cowered in fear while this unfolded. Surprisingly, Travis gave up all of his belongings without ant resistance.

What really shocked us is that the dudes who robbed him thanked him for posting where he was. They didn't harm him or any of us who were in White Castle at the time. The gunmen didn't even rob anyone else or tell the cashiers to empty the register. They were in and out in no time.   Once they ran out the door, they disappeared into the darkness of the night. Travis has never been able to live that down.

I begin cracking jokes on the rest of the guys who were laughing at me. I embarrass all of them as we walk to school. We make it to school and the jokes stop because we all disperse. They'll think twice about trying to roast me. We get to homeroom and I remember that I have a few questions to answer for an assignment I was supposed to do for homework.   I'm glad I remembered it because I would have hated to get to first period and not have it done. I know that there's no excuse for not having my work done especially when I've been hanging out all weekend. Not having my work done may have been justified if I was sick, but that wasn't my case.   I read and answer the questions of the assignment feverishly. Just as the dismissal bell from homeroom sounds, I complete the last question. I'm prepared for first period!

I walk into first period class and get my work out. I've never been a person who needs to be prompted to do what I'm supposed to do. However, that's not the case for a lot of people. Several of my classmates come into class as the bell is ringing and sit down. There's light chatter as they take their seats and then my boy Justin realizes he doesn't have his work for today.

"Damn, I forgot about the reading assignment. Chris, I know you got ya work done. I'm about to copy yours real quick," Justin says.

I reply, "You know I have my work done because I always do, but you also know that I don't let anyone copy my work."

"Bruh, Come on! Son, it'll only be this one time... on everything. I can't take another zero or late penalty. I'll copy it and give it right back to you. I'll even get a couple answers wrong, so the teacher doesn't think we copied each other's work," Justin states.

"I feel you, but it's not happening. If the teacher sees you with my work, we're both getting zeros and I'm not chancing it. Bruh, ain't no way I'm getting a zero for work I've done. You're bugging. Keeping it real, you shouldn't even be asking me for my work knowing the potential consequences. You could be throwing me under the bus," I orate.

"Damn, if I woulda known you were gonna give me a lecture, I woulda never asked. Fuck it, don't even worry about it. I'm good," Justin shoots back angrily.

Justin walks off and I don't respond. They say there's no need to argue with a fool, so I won't. Also, he's clearly upset with me, so there's no need to respond. I could potentially be throwing fuel on an open flame. I don't get why he's so mad because I've never shared my work with him. It's not like he's incapable of doing the work, he just chooses not to. I'm not participating in his laziness and lack of discipline.

Maybe one day he'll get his mind right.

The teacher takes attendance and then we begin the instructional part of class. The teacher has us taking notes that she has posted on the board. From the notes, we have to look up some things on the internet to help with our understanding of the topic. We finish that and then go over the homework assignment we had. Every time the teacher asks a question, the same people raise their hands. Only four of us answer the questions. My teacher doesn't like the fact that we're dominating the class discussion, so she calls on people who haven't had their hand raised.

She calls on several people who are seemingly disinterested in the conversation. We all know that most of the people who don't want to answer questions is because they didn't do the assignment. Unfortunately, some of our classmates have other reasons why they won't raise their hands. Some of them haven't slept much and are just dead tired and someone else doesn't feel well, so he just has his head down. A few students who didn't raise their hands actually answered questions correctly and added value to the class discussion. Class is going smoothly until Mrs. Johnston calls on Terrance.

"Terrance, answer question six for us please," she states.

Terrance answers question six correctly. Mrs. Johnston likes his answer so much that she admits that she hadn't thought of that perspective before. Next, she asks him what part of the passage we had to read sent him in that direction of thinking. Unfortunately, Terrance is unable to answer her question. In fact, he freezes like a deer in headlights. Seconds later, he looks in the book and then starts talking about the passage instead of reading it verbatim.

The only problem with that is that he's not making any sense. The teacher stops him in his broken and obfuscated explanation and just tells him to read the passage related to his answer. Sadly, he is unable to do so. The only reason he got the question right is because I gave him the answer. I let him copy my answers because he can't read very well. He reads on a fifth-grade level and the text we use is written for twelfth grade. I help him out as much as I can because his situation is dire unlike Justin who is just plain lazy.

All of our classmates know that Terrance doesn't read very well and we feel sorry for him. Mrs. Johnston doesn't care about his situation because if she did, she wouldn't be pushing him so hard. Mrs. Johnston orders him to read the passage, but he won't. I can tell Terrance is becoming frustrated by her dictation. I just hope he doesn't snap on her.

"Terrance, if you did the work yourself, there's no reason why you shouldn't read the passage," Mrs. Johnston says.

"I don't want to read the damn passage. This

shit is wack as hell! That's why I don't want to read it," yells Terrance as he slams the book shut and swipes it off of his desk.

"Umm, you need to pick up that book now and watch your mouth. You need to apologize to me and your classmates for that outburst or I'm going to have to remove you from class," Mrs. Johnston orders sternly.

Terrance seems to not hear what Mrs. Johnston says because he isn't answering or moving to pick the book up. We're all sure he did hear her though because the teacher wasn't using her inside voice when she gave him the directive. Terrance is sitting in his chair with his arms folded as if he doesn't have a care in the world. However, his facial expression clearly indicates that he is livid.

"Terrance, did you hear me? Do you want me to have you removed from class?" Mrs. Johnston interrogates.

After Terrance rolls his eyes and sucks his teeth, he answers, "Yeah, I heard you. If you wanna kick me out, go ahead and do it because I really don't care. All they gonna do is send me to in-school for the rest of the day. That's better than reading this boring assignment."

Mrs. Johnston doesn't like his apathy towards her threat to put him out of class. For some reason, she thought Terrance was going to be influenced to do what she wanted him to do. The last thing Terrance cares about is being removed from class. Mrs. Johnston makes good on her promise and orders Terrance out of the class. He promptly gets up and puts his book bag on. As he walks through the row, he bumps several desks and causes quite a bit of clamor. This is his final act of defiance as he leaves the classroom.

The students in the class have mixed emotions about what just went down. I think they both were at fault. In my opinion, Mrs. Johnston was at fault because she knows Terrance's situation. Almost everyone in the class knows the situation Terrance is in. Unfortunately, Terrance doesn't read very well either. He always stumbles through anything he reads and also doesn't comprehend very well. According to him, he only reads at a fifth-grade level. That's why I say Mrs. Johnston is partially to blame for what happened. She should have never called on him to read knowing his educational deficiencies.

Even if she initially forgot about his situation, once she realized her blunder, she should have called on someone else. There was no need for her to continue pushing him like that. However, Terrance is not without blame either. He could have handled the situation better too. All he had to do was decline to read as he's done many times before. There was no reason for him to blow up in class like that. I'm sure he just wanted to mask the fact that he's poor at reading. He probably thought that acting up would hide the true problem. Two wrongs definitely don't make a right.

Class has been interrupted for no reason. The teacher gets on the classroom phone and calls an administrator to let him know what transpired. The teacher directs us to do some silent reading while she writes a referral for Terrance. This is a total waste of class time. It takes the class a few minutes to settle down, but we calm our nerves and get to work.

REFLECTION

Terrance is in high school, but sadly only reads on a fifth-grade level. Unfortunately, this is not a fictitious happening. This type of thing is running rampant throughout the high schools in this country. The truth is that nothing is really being done to erase the problem and to keep it from happening again. Why do I say this? I feel this way because students are tested from their early days in school. Many students perform poorly in school and if you track their progress throughout their entire school career, you'll see the growth is minimal. I used to work at a community center with kids. One of my duties at the community center was to help kids with their homework. I was able to see who was struggling with reading and who wasn't. As fate would have it, years later, I ended up teaching in the same school district that the community center was in. I became the English teacher of many of the students who were members of the community center I formerly worked at.

I was dumbfounded when it became evident that the same students who struggled with reading at the community center years earlier, were the same students who had problems reading in my class. How is it possible for a student to go through years of schooling and not learn how to read on their appropriate grade level? The next question is what is the true goal of education? Reading is at the foundation of education, so it seems like that would be the most important thing taught in school.

We also know that students who can't perform to the standards set in school often become discipline problems to mask their educational deficiencies. Almost everything students have to do in class involves reading, so it's inexcusable that so many kids are poor readers. The blame doesn't solely rest on the school system. Of course, parents have to play a part in their kid's education, but we know they often don't. I'm a former educator and I feel the burden then falls on the schools to ensure children receive adequate education.

What can the schools do? They can do plenty to solve the problem. The first thing is to use the data they collect more efficiently. Data is collected in schools, but how to use the data effectively is where problems arise. School districts pay experts to come in once or twice a year to instruct others on how to use the data and then they're gone. Teachers are left with inadequate training on how to use the data properly. Proper training for teachers is key. Teachers really aren't trained to contend with the millions of issues they face in the classroom. A teacher may be an expert in their discipline, but are required to collect and analyze data that's totally outside his or her area of expertise.

Teachers are only a small fraction of the problem. The most important part of this dilemma is the students. Students are identified early on as struggling students, so it doesn't make sense that years later they're still struggling. If anything is being done to change their at-risk status, it isn't working. A system driven by test scores is missing the true goal of school. The goal should be to graduate students who can be productive citizens. Students who don't read on their grade level should be targeted by the education team in an effort to get the kids' skills up. How can this be accomplished?

Once students are tested, their results need to be analyzed. The results will clearly show who needs remediation and who does not. At that point, it would be time to implement all of the proven effective reading strategies. Students whose scores don't fall in a certain range should be removed from classes such as art, gym, Spanish, and any other classes that don't promote their reading levels rising. I would do this because the schools need to maximize the amount of remediation students get. Kids are only in school for a limited number of hours, so you have to use each minute wisely. Also, students will most likely work harder to get their skills up because they know they'll be able to return to the "fun" classes once they do. Passing struggling students along with no real attempt to help them only creates lifelong struggles in school and potentially after school. Nothing can justify a student's reading level not growing any after years of schooling.

CHAPTER 11
Kennedy's Perspective

I'm so glad today went by so quickly. If the days keep going this fast, Chris and I will be graduating in no time. Chris is walking some girl he likes home today, so I'm walking home by myself. It's no big deal for me to walk home alone because I only live a stone's throw away. While I'm walking out of the school building, I see two girls that I'm cool with from gym class.

"Hey, Kennedy. I know you're not walking home without ya brother," says Kayla.

Corrin adds her two cents, "I know right. I don't think I've ever seen you walking home without ya cute ass brother."

"Girl, y'all crazy. I don't always be with my brother. Don't try my life," I state as I laugh.

Kayla speaks, "The hell y'all ain't always together. I know you two are twins, but I see you and ya brother together so much that I started thinking y'all were Siamese twins or something."

"I'm not messing with y'all. Y'all cray cray. I walked home without my brother one day last week too," I reply.

"Shit, maybe you did, but I ain't see ya ass. I ain't gonna lie… I wish he was with you right now," Corrin adds.

We are all walking the same direction, so I walk with them as they make lewd comments about my brother. I find their remarks comical and they don't bother me. I already knew that Corrin and Kayla liked my brother. Many other girls at school are feeling my brother too and I'm used to hearing what they'd do to him sexually if they had the chance. The girls want to stop by the corner store before they head home, so we head that way.

We walk into the corner store and the girls grab a few things and are even nice enough to cop me a couple of snacks. I didn't ask for them, but I wasn't going to refuse them either. They pay for the snacks and we walk out. We head up Bigelow Ave. and a car with a girl we all know pulls up. The girl's name is Meesha and she graduated two years ago.

Meesha got pregnant during her senior year, but didn't let her pregnancy keep her from graduating high school. Meesha sees us as she's parking the car and is waving at us frantically. She was always cool with me and was never on any funny stuff. Although we were cool in school, I hadn't seen her since she graduated. I saw some pictures of her and her baby on The Gram, but that's about it. It's still all love though, we just lost touch. She's moving her way and I'm moving mine.

Meesha jumps out of the car as soon as she parks and practically runs over to us. She's just as excited to see us as we are to see her. We share in some short embraces as her child's father gets out the car and goes in the store. Meesha catches us up to speed on what's been going on with her and we do the same. The conversation is all laughs and positive statements. Meesha's son is in the car and we want to see him. For this reason, Meesha pulls her son out of his car seat and out of the car.

"Girl, he is so adorable!" I comment. "He has your dimples too."

"Thank you girl! Everybody says that he's my twin, but his daddy don't wanna admit it," Meesha says.

Corrin words, "He is definitely your twin. I mean like a spitting image and he is so cute. I like his braids."

Kayla asks, "What's his name?"

"His name is Elijah. Girl, he is bad as hell. I tell you," Meesha voices.

"You know boys are always all over da place! Can't sit still!" Kayla verbalizes.

"Girl, you ain't never lied. I swear Elijah was

just being born like last week and now he's running around the house," Meesha states.

Corrin says, "He's gonna be a heartbreaker. I can tell already. Look how cute he is and he has good hair!"

"Yes, my little man is going to be a heartbreaker. I can tell these little girls gonna be acting stupid over him in a few years," Meesha suggests.

I listen as they go back and forth about Elijah. Finally, they switch the conversation about how cute Elijah is to talking about going to school. Meesha is studying nursing at Essex County College and tells us not to get pregnant until we're out of school and financially stable. A few minutes later, her child's father emerges from the corner store. Meesha introduces him to us and he gets back in the car.

To my surprise, my brother turns the corner from Elizabeth Ave. and walks up to us. I guess he wasn't being nasty with the girl he walked home from school today. Corrin and Kayla immediately greet him and are very warm to him. Chris speaks back, but then his attention is taken by Meesha's baby daddy. Her baby daddy is in the car going crazy because he and Chris are cool, but they haven't seen each other in a long time. He gets out of the car and gives Chris a dap and a manly hug. They're all smiles as they talk loudly.

"Yo, I ain't seen you in forever!" Chris says excitedly.

Donavan replies, "I know fam. Son, it's been mad long!"

"What's been good? What you been into?" Chris asks.

"Shit, just taking care of my seed. That's my little nigga right there. Elijah, say what up to Chris. Give him a pound like I taught you to," says Donavan. "He gonna pull mad chicks like I used to."

Little Elijah does as his father tells him to do and gives Chris a pound. We all stand around talking. Meesha brings up that she heard Chris beat up Mark pretty badly, but my brother downplays it like he normally does. Donavan gives Chris props for beating Mark up. He states that he saw the video of the fight. Chris changes the subject immediately. He doesn't want to stir up more beef with Mark through them.

We all talk for a few more minutes and then Meesha and Donavan pull off. Donavan and my brother claim that they're going to hang out soon, but I know they aren't. If they haven't linked up in all of this time, I know they aren't all of a sudden going to start chilling now. Meesha also states that she's going to hit me up, but I'm not really too pressed to hang with her. The way I see it is that we lost touch for a reason, so we should let it stay that way. We had good times in the past, but now it's the present. She's just not a part of my current situation.

Corrin and Kayla make slick comments to

my brother while we walk up the block. He brushes their comments off all the way to our house. They both tell my brother that they're going to Snap him later. He doesn't tell them not to, so I assume that he wants their attention.

"Are you really gonna chill with Meesha?" Chris asks.

"Bruh, hell no! I don't even know her anymore. It was good seeing her, but I'm good on that. I'm definitely not going to hit her up. I'll just see her on social media," I answer.

"True, I asked because you know I don't plan on hitting Donavan up either. You know me and you are always on the same wavelength. I can tell his mind isn't right," Chris verbalizes.

I respond, "I already know what you're going to say. Your mouth damn near dropped when he called his son a little nigga. I was tripping inside when he said that. I couldn't believe it."

"I wasn't going to say anything to him, but I thought that was out of line, but that's not my son or my place to say anything," Chris states. "I couldn't wait to talk to you about it. I was hoping Corrin and Kayla left us sooner. I damn sure wasn't going to say anything in front of them and then they go back and tell. Before you know it, I'd have beef with Donavan."

I voice, "To each his own. It's not our place to say anything. Plus, you know people tend to be overly sensitive when it pertains to their kids. Corrin and Kayla would be telling everybody what we said, while we were saying it. They probably woulda went live while we were talking."

"I know, right. They definitely talk too much. Sis, I can't believe he called his son a nigga like that. Out of all the positive terms in the world to call a child, he picks a negative term. I don't get it. I'd never call my son a nigga or any form of it," Chris speaks.

"You know you don't have to tell me. I was right there with you. People need to be extremely careful with the terms the use to call their children by. I've seen it go badly too many times. Once a kid gets labeled, it can be extremely hard to shed it," I recite.

Chris and I talk about the school day like we always do. His phone rings and he answers it. Our conversation is over, so I go into the bathroom and comb my hair. I hear my brother on the phone laughing with his boy and giving him advice. That's my brother. He's always level headed and willing to offer his advice when he can. I love my brother and he loves me. We're always there for one another. It's he and I against the world.

The day quickly turns to night. My brother decides to get out his clothes for tomorrow, so I follow his lead. He irons my clothes after he finishes his. I make us both some grilled cheese sandwiches for dinner and then we take it down.

REFLECTION

We need to be extremely careful with the terms we use to describe ourselves and our kids especially. We need to be prudent in the words we ascribe to people because the ramifications of not being prudent can have harmful effects. The human psyche is fragile for adults and even more impressionable for children. Therefore, all words and descriptors should be carefully thought out before given to children. How exactly can labels hurt a child?

The answer to how labeling children can be harmful is worthy of discussion. One can't readily predict how it will impact a child because people respond to things differently. For example, the child in this scenario was called a heartbreaker. We know that this most likely means that the child is cute and adorable. They call the child a heartbreaker because experience tells them that the child will grow up to be liked by many women. Of course, the problem is not that the child is cute. However, the problem is that he's being called a heartbreaker. This is suggestive that he'll have many girlfriends and they'll be in love with him. The term heartbreaker means that the boy will leave the women who love him heartbroken. It's possible that when the boy learns what the term means, he'll become just that. Why wouldn't he if he's been referred to that all of his life? He may grow up thinking that being a heartbreaker is perfectly fine. Unfortunately, misogynistic tendencies are highly favored in some cultures.

As stated, words can carry weight with irreversible impacts. In many circles, the word nigga is also seen as a negative term and can also have negative mental impacts on the child, but what society considers positive words can also have a poor influence on children. Many people would argue how positive words can be harmful and it makes sense. It seems like positive attributes would be a great idea, but it may not be.

Many people refer to their children as a king, a prince, or the man of the house. On the surface those words seem harmless. They actually appear to be positive words. There's nothing wrong with calling a kid a man or a king, right? I beg to differ and suggest that these terms and others like them can be just as harmful as terms that most would consider negative terms. Why do I say that?

Unless we're in a monarchy, there are no kings, queens, princesses, or princes, so using those terms is actually a misrepresentation. It can become harmful to the child because he or she is being given a status that has yet to be attained. The child has put forth no effort to have a label of such high esteem. If you call a boy a man, he may think that being a man is just something that is given to him, but doesn't require effort or responsibility. Why would he think he's a man when he's not? He would think that because he has nothing of his own, but has always been referred to as a man or a king. The person is going to eventually get to the age where he is a man and potentially never do the things that men do because he's been told for many years that he's already a man. Essentially, his definition of a man is altered or skewed. His mother fixed him food, took care of him, and washed his clothes while calling him the man of the house or a king. Why wouldn't he think that a man is a person who gets provided for instead of doing the providing?

It doesn't matter whether a term is considered positive or negative because they both can have negative effects. I'd be misleading if I said that it's not possible for the same words to have positive impacts on kids. My point is that we should tread carefully when hurling terms at children. We really should refer to them as what they are. They are children, boys and girls and should be referred to as such. For example, let's say a parent wants their child to have a high paying career such as a doctor. However, the child is only six years old and in the first grade. The parent would never go around telling people that her son or daughter is a doctor. If the parent did ascribe those credentials to the child, he or she would be totally off base. The reason the parent would be amiss is because the child is not a doctor or anything close to it.

Now, what the parent should do is speak in terms of the future. In order to be a doctor, there are things you have to do first. It's not a title that's given; it's earned. With that being said, I wouldn't call my son a man when he's only six years old. I would tell him that he'll be a man one day when he does certain things. He has to meet certain criteria to become a man. This opens up the conversation for what a man is and what a man does. The parent will be able to train him to become a man just as a person trains to become a doctor. The subtleties in the things we say can make a world of difference in the outcome. Be mindful with the words we use to describe our kids.

CHAPTER 12
Christopher's Perspective

What time is it? I know it's mad early. Why does she have the music blasting? I know she could listen to the music through her headphones. It's Saturday morning and she knows that I normally sleep late. Not that I sleep until three o'clock in the afternoon, but it's only eight thirty. I didn't go to sleep until three, so I wanted to sleep until at least eleven. Shoot, studies say that we should get about eight hours of sleep each night and I was attempting to do just that.

I don't get out the bed to tell her to kill the music because I know that once I get out of the bed, I'm up for good. Instead, I send Kennedy a text to turn the music down or to put her ear buds in. A few minutes transpire and I still don't receive a message back from her. I know she's not ignoring my text. I can even see that she read the message. She actually left me on read! That's foul. I'm still not getting out the bed, so I text her again to get at her for not hitting me back.

Again, she doesn't respond. Seconds later, Kennedy bursts into my room as if she owns the place. It's not the first time she's done this, so I don't even get mad. She's lucky I wasn't in here naked or anything. She would have been scarred for life. It would have served her right for coming in without knocking. I've warned her on several occasions, but she continues to burst right in. She's better than me because I have never and will never burst into her room unannounced.

"Yo, what you want? Why you blowing my phone up like you a damn female?" Kennedy shoots at me.

"I wanted you to turn the music down. Don't act like you didn't see my text. You left me on read, so I know you saw it. I wouldn't have had to blow ya phone up if you woulda responded to my first text," I defend.

"Yeah, whatever. That music wasn't that loud and if it woke you up, I'm glad. You need to get ya ass up," Kennedy states.

"Son, that music was what woke me up. I definitely don't need to get up yet. It's stupid early," I speak.

"That was the point of me blasting it. I wanted to wake you up, so we can get on the move. I ain't trying to wait all day," Kennedy words.

I have no idea why she cares about waking me up and I surely don't know where we're supposed to get on the move to. All I know is that's it's eight thirty in the morning and I can use some more sleep. Truth be told, there isn't anywhere to go this early anyway. I know Kennedy's not trying to go jogging in the park. Either way, I'm not getting up right now.

I ask, "Umm, what are we supposedly getting on the move for?"

Kennedy answers, "I knew you were gonna forget. I told you that I wanted you to go downtown with me, so I can get an outfit for Shakeerah's 18th birthday party tonight. You're bugging because I just reminded you again on Thursday!"

"Oh shit! Damn, that is right. Yo, I'm tripping because I forgot all about that. Give me like another hour or two and I'll be ready. I'm tired as hell," I vocalize, while pulling my cover back over my head.

"I know you forgot, but I'm not waiting another hour or two to go downtown. We gotta catch the bus and ain't no telling how late the buses will start running as the day goes on. I'm not trying to be out there all day waiting for the 59 to pull up," Kennedy replies forcefully.

I say, "You being way extra. The 59 bus stop is right there and we'll be downtown in like ten minutes. We can be in and out. Give me an hour."

"Hell no! You said you were going with me, so come now or don't worry about it. I still gotta go get my hair done too. I'm going without you if you don't want to go with me now," Kennedy articulates. "You shouldn't have said that you'd be ready whenever I wanted to go."

I really want to stay in the bed and get some more sleep, but I did tell her that I'd be ready whenever she wanted to go. I guess I shouldn't have spoken so freely or maybe I should've gone to sleep earlier. I never leave my sister hanging, so I know I have to get up and go. She doesn't say anything else and exits my room. She's head strong, so I know she's really going to leave without me. I go to my bedroom door and inform her that I'll be ready in a few minutes. She smiles and goes into her room.

I skip taking a shower and just do a quick washing up at the sink. It isn't the first time that I've delayed taking a shower and it won't be the last. I hear Kennedy calling my name, so I know she's ready to go. She yells out to me again and I hear her saying the bus is coming in ten minutes and she's ready to go. I grab my phone off the charger and we walk out the house. As soon as we get to the sidewalk, we see the bus we need to catch stopped at the red light. We can't miss the bus because the next one isn't until ten thirty, so we take off running to catch it. The light changes as we approach the bus stop. We dodge two cars while crossing the street, but we make it to the bus stop just before the bus does.

"You know I woulda been mad at you if we missed the bus. You're lucky as hell!" Kennedy states.

"That ain't bout nothing cause we didn't miss the bus. Chill with that madness," I respond.

The bus makes its normal stops and we get downtown in no time. We get off the bus just as the stores are opening. I'm not going to the birthday party tonight, so I'm not getting anything. I'm really just helping my sister pick out something dope for the party. I heard it's supposed to be lit, but I didn't get an invitation until late. Plus, a lot of dudes won't talk to my sister when I'm around. I don't want to cramp her style, so I'll sit this one out.

We are at the intersection of Broad and Market Streets when Kennedy starts walking towards Dr. Jays. I don't know why she even acted like she wanted to go in another store first. She always goes in Dr. Jays first when we shop, but acts like she's going somewhere else. We walk into the store and she beelines for the women's section. I look at a couple snapbacks and then join her. She looks at several items and gets my opinion on them. After an hour of trying things on, she picks out a fresh outfit. I completely cosign her copping it. She already has some red shoes to go with the dress, so she buys that and we bounce.

We leave the store and walk back to the bus stop. Kennedy is happy because we're leaving pretty rapidly. Most times she takes much longer to find an outfit than she did today. She knows the saved time will aid her going forward because she'll be able to get her hair done sooner. I'm perfectly fine with getting from down here quickly because I'm trying to get back home, so I can get in the bed. We walk back to the bus stop and wait for the bus. Our timing is perfect because the 59 is supposed to be here in a few minutes.

To our delight, the bus is on schedule. We board the bus and head back to the house. The bus stops at its normal stops. My sister and I talk as we ride. She claims that she's going to be the most popping person at the party. Even if she's really not, I'm sure she'll report that she is anyway. We all have a tendency to over represent ourselves. I can't front like I'm not guilty of it myself. The bus makes another stop near Clinton Ave. to pick up more people. Several people get off the bus and others get on.

"Damn! Look Kennedy," I say.

She asks, "What?"

I don't respond to her because she turns and sees who just boarded the bus. Unfortunately, Mark just got on the bus. I haven't had any close contact with him lately and I hope he doesn't become hostile toward me. I tell Kennedy not to look at him because he may take that gesture as a taunt. She looks away as I asked her to, but I can't take my eyes off of him. I don't want to taunt him either, but I don't want to turn my back on him and he uses that to his advantage. For all I know, he may try to jump on me while my back is to him.

He walks past us and stares at me viciously. I see hate in his eyes, but he isn't saying anything to us, so his stares don't bother me. I can't wait to get off this bus. Our stop is almost here, but I'm sure it'll seemingly take an eternity to reach. Mark won't take his eyes off of us and it's making me more uncomfortable by the moment.

I say to Kennedy, "Yo, we should get off the bus now. I think it's better to get away from Mark. The longer we are near him, the more likely it is that something will happen."

"Okay, I'm ready when you are," Kennedy replies.

I decide not to wait until the next stop. We are close enough to our place to walk from here. I approach the bus driver and fake sick. I know if I tell him that I just want to exit the bus before the stop, he'll not grant my request. Life has taught me that sometimes you have to use a little bit of deceit to get what you want. I fake as if I'm going to throw up and he stops the bus immediately and opens the door.

"Your bitch ass better get off the bus before I fuck ya ass up! Tell ya thotty body ass sister to get the fuck off the bus," Mark yells angrily.

I tell Kennedy to come on. She walks toward me and I let her exit the bus first. Mark jumps up as I'm walking down the bus steps and swings at me. What a sucker he is. Fortunately, I saw it coming, so I was able to get out the way of most of the hit. His hand barely grazes the side of my face. I decide not to fight back and try to get off the bus, but he grabs me and we start fighting on the steps. I get the upper hand on him and punch him a few times before several people pull us apart. When things get sorted out, the bus driver puts Mark off of the bus because he initiated the fight. Kennedy is back on the bus and we head to our seats.

Mark mean mugs us as the bus pulls off. The unthinkable happens as we begin to gain speed. Mark runs alongside the bus, pulls out a shiny pistol, and lets off several shots into the bus. Many people on the bus scream in fear, while others cry in panic. We all get down trying to avoid getting hit by the bullets. Glass shards fly everywhere as the bullets shatter the windows. Finally, the bus is away from Mark.

I begin to get up along with many of the other bus passengers. As I stand, I realize that there's blood on me and glass all over me. I'm extremely befuddled by how much blood is on me. I know it's highly likely that I got cut by some of the flying glass, but this is too much blood for that. Someone has to be hit. To my horror, I don't see Kennedy standing up. I immediately feel a sharp pain in my stomach as I look behind me on the floor. Kennedy isn't standing because she's been shot and is bleeding profusely.

I drop to the floor to tend to her. I call her name, while I investigate where she's bleeding from. It looks like she was shot in the stomach because that's where all of the blood is staining her shirt. The bus driver stops the bus to come help out. Several people call 911 to hopefully get some medical assistance here. My sister is unconscious and isn't responding to anything I'm saying or asking. Honestly, I can't tell if she's dead or alive. One of the ladies on the bus is a registered nurse and is helping as much as she can. She's pressing Kennedy's stomach to keep pressure on the wound.

"Fuck! Fuck! Fuck! Don't die Kennedy. Please don't die! This is all my fault! Fuck! I got my sister shot!" I scream as I pound on one of the bus seats.

Everyone on the bus is telling me that it's not my fault, but I don't want to hear it. The way I see it, it is my fault. If I didn't have the fight with Mark, we would never have been beefing. Therefore, Mark wouldn't have fought me on the bus today and wouldn't have shot my sister. Maybe I should have let him beat me up today or even at the football game. If he would've won or thought he won, my sister wouldn't be lying here on the floor of a bus bleeding all over the place.

It's tough when you can't even defend yourself in a fair and square fashion and have that be the end of it. You really have to consider if allowing yourself to be victimized is your best option. If you win a fight, you have to worry about a person coming back to shoot you. If you lose a fight on purpose, you have to carry the burden of knowing you didn't defend yourself to the best of your ability. Additionally, you have to encounter all of the criticism from the spectators of the fight. They'll surely ridicule you for losing the fight and possibly try to fight you as well. Unfortunately, it becomes a never ending cycle.

You're damned if you do and damned if you don't. That's why I do my best to avoid drama, gossip, and conflict all the time. If Mark wouldn't have attacked me, I would have never fought him. The worst part about it is that it's all over a stolen bike. With the way things are today, it's almost like you're better off shooting a person who wants to fight you from the onset of the problem because he'll shoot you if you beat him up. If someone has to die, it might as well be the other person.

The cops and ambulance are on the scene and are assisting my sister. The ambulance personnel are able to get Kennedy's pulse, but it's weak. She's not dead and is fighting for her life. There are no words that have ever been created that can describe the way I feel right now. The emergency officials have my sister in their emergency vehicle and are taking her to Beth Israel Hospital. The cops are taking statements from everyone. They attempt to get my statement, but I get in the emergency vehicle to ride to the hospital. They'll have to talk to me down there because there is no way that I'm leaving my sister's side.

We quickly arrive at the hospital and they rush Kennedy into emergency surgery. Moments later, while I'm in the waiting room, the police come in to interview me. Nobody on the bus knew Mark's identity other than Kennedy and me. They ask me if I know the suspect's name and I freeze momentarily. I don't freeze because I'm worried about being labeled as a snitch, but I do freeze because I know if I give the authorities his name, they'll go pick him up and arrest him.

I surely want Mark to pay for the crime he's committed, but I haven't decided how I want him to pay. He may need to suffer street justice from my hands. I might like that better than him being behind bars. I know I won't have an opportunity to get revenge if they lock him up. I have to buy myself some time. The cop asks me again if I know the shooter.

"Alright, I'm not gonna lie. I do know the shooter. We used to be pretty cool with one another," I answer.

The cop words, "It goes like that sometimes. All friendships don't last forever, but it's good you know his identity, so we can hurry up and get him off the streets and make him pay for harming your sister. Just tell me his name and I'll get right to finding him."

"It's not that simple. I don't want to be called

a snitch. You know that snitches get stitches. That's the code of the streets. I'll be in danger if I do that. I might get shot from one of the hood dudes," I state.

"I know the so-called code of the streets, but that's your sister he shot. You owe her more than you owe anyone else, so I advise you to give me his name," voices the cop.

I know he's one hundred percent correct about owing my sister, but he doesn't know my true intention and I can't reveal it to him. The truth is that I'm not scared of the people in the streets. I want the cops to go find another way to find out who did it. That'll give me time to find Mark and make him pay for what he's done.

"Officer, you may have to look at the cameras on the bus to get his name because I don't know if I should tell on him. I'm not a rat," I verbalize.

The officer is visibly angry at me and attempts to get me to tell him Mark's name one more time, but I don't. The cop leaves to chase down Mark's identity by other means. I have to settle the score. Mark turned up by shooting my sister. Well, I can turn up too. My turn up game is way strong. I'm going to have to set it off. I have to defend my sister. Besides, if I don't kill him, he's going to kill me. He's proven that he will. I pull my phone out of my pocket and make a call and my boy Brandon answers.

"Yo, what's good?" Brandon asks as he answers the phone.

"Shit, is crazy as hell right now. My sister got shot on some crazy shit while we were on the bus coming from downtown," I answer.

Brandon speaks angrily and shocked, "Yo, get the fuck outta here! I know she ain't dead!"

I state, "Nah, she's not, but she's in surgery now. They said they don't know how it's gonna turn out though."

"Damn, who did that shit?" Brandon inquires.

"Bitch ass Mark did it. We saw him on the bus and he swung on me, so I fucked him up again. Before you know it, he was letting off. Shit was crazy as hell! Son, I need ya help though," I verbalize.

"Mark would be the one to do it. I should've known he did it. He's been salty ever since you beat him up the first time. Bruh, I'm sorry to hear that. Say the word and whatever you need is yours. I got you!" Brandon replies.

"Word. Good looking out. Yo, I need short sleeves and I know you always bear arms. I gotta settle the score for myself and my sister. Ain't no more fighting," I orate.

"You ain't said nothing, but a word. Come through my cousin crib on Renner and I got you," Brandon states.

I leave the hospital immediately to head over to Renner Ave. The hospital is only a couple blocks away, so I don't mind walking. I get to Brandon's house and walk inside. Brandon shows me a few different guns and tells me that I can pick which one I want. I'm not a gun aficionado, so I grab a revolver that he has. It's a thirty-eight and will do the job just fine. Brandon tells me that I need to dump the gun once I use it. He doesn't want any part of a gun with a body on it.

I leave Brandon's house with the gun tucked in my waist. I figure Mark has to make it back to his crib at some point, so I go over to his block to wait for him. Maybe he isn't dumb enough to come back here. He might think that I told the cops his name and knows that the police would come here first. While I'm waiting, my phone starts vibrating in my pocket. I reach to retrieve my phone and see that it's Brandon.

I answer the phone and say, "Yo."

"Son, I don't know where you're at, but I heard that Mark is heading to North Eleventh to hide out. Dude I'm cool with is about to take him over there now," Brandon reports.

"You serious? Did ya peoples say where he's at now?" I ask.

"Yeah, I'm dead ass serious. He said he was picking him up on Nye Ave," Brandon answers.

"Alright! That's good because I'm on Nye now two houses down from Mark's crib," I say.

While I'm talking to Brandon I see a car turn onto the block and is creeping toward Mark's crib. The car is a black Camry. I can tell the driver is looking for someone or something. Unfortunately, the car passes Mark's crib and goes to the next block, so I figure the driver must be looking for someone else. The driver of the car is just sitting in the street waiting for a second. Something doesn't seem right.

"Brandon, are you still there? Do you know what kind of car ya boy has?" I inquire.

He answers, "Yeah, he got a black Camry."

I say, "Hell yeah! That's him then. Yo, I'm gonna holla back. I'm bout to light his ass up on everything!"

I don't wait for Brandon to reply before I end the call. I move stealthily to the next block. I hold my position near where the Camry is sitting to see if Mark comes out from anywhere. The driver of the Camry probably didn't pull up to Mark's crib directly because Mark most likely doesn't want to be caught there. I see the driver make a phone call and then pops the trunk. Next, I see Mark emerge from the backyard of one of the houses. He heads to the trunk of the car and goes to jump in it. As he is climbing into the trunk, I flash out from my hiding spot with my gun drawn and run up on him. Mark's cornered between the trunk of the car and me. As the song reads, "Y'all respect the one who got shot, I respect the shooter."

"Now what nigga!" I scream.

REFLECTION

Unfortunately, the situation with Mark is far too common in our neighborhoods. Many small situations grow into huge and sometimes deadly situations. We all know that anyone can fight. You may not be able to fight well, but anyone can fight. It doesn't take any thought to harm someone. People have dogs and cats fighting all the time, so it can't be anything too profound about fighting, but for some reason it's highly favored in our culture.

Something needs to happen in order to change the minds of this generation where fighting is their answer for seemingly every disagreement. What exactly needs to happen to change this overly confrontational generation? I've seen countless videos on social media where parents were teaching their children how to defend themselves. They purchased boxing gloves and other materials to aid in the process of teaching their children how to fight. Don't get me wrong, I think that has merit because you want your children to know how to defend themselves if a situation comes to that.

However, there is more to defending yourself than just fighting. The physical altercation is the very last option on the list of things to do when it pertains to disagreements. Even though fighting should be the last thing that happens, it is normally the first thing that occurs. We're constantly bombarded with fight videos being shared on social media. I've even seen videos on social media where community members have stated an initiative to thwart shooting violence. That's a good idea to some degree because we definitely want to stop all violence in our communities, especially senseless gun violence. This initiative calls for people with disagreements to put on boxing gloves to settle their disputes instead of using guns.

Putting guns down and picking boxing gloves up is great when you compare one violent act to the other, but fighting is not what we should want our kids to be doing. Again, fighting is a last resort. There is a key element missing in our communities when it comes to our youth fighting one another. Well, what's missing? What's missing is education. Children are not being educated properly when it comes to fighting.

Young kids often complain about being disrespected, but haven't been properly schooled on what disrespect is. I've seen students have disagreements about sports, clothes, and even television shows and then claim someone disrespected them. Kids often mistake differing opinions with being disrespected and that's clearly not disrespect. Their differing opinions often lead to name calling and talking behind one another's backs. Shortly thereafter, physical confrontations ensue. If our youth are taught a clear definition of what disrespect is and given scenarios, they'll be better equipped to deal with real life instances if they occur. They are also missing many valuable lessons on what being respectful is to begin with.

What needs to be promulgated is the most important part of any conflict situation. This key piece of teaching or education should be what we see the most when dealing with conflicts. What is needed one might ask? Our youth need to be well versed in conflict avoidance. Having conflict avoidance skills will enable kids to bypass potential conflict situations before they occur because they'll know signs that often lead to conflict. The next step in the progression of dealing with conflict is conflict diffusion. Unfortunately, all conflict can't be avoided, but it is possible to diffuse conflicts before it is exacerbated. People often add fuel to the flame of conflict by indulging in behaviors that promote conflict. For example, they'll taunt the other person or spread gossip about the other individual. This is totally adversarial to conflict diffusion. Our youth need to be taught to keep their involvement in conflict to a minimum instead of the maximum. While teaching the youth how to defend themselves is a good idea and is needed, it sends the wrong message if how to fight is the only thing being taught. Again, fighting is a last resort and should be avoided whenever possible.

EPILOGUE

We all want our kids to succeed, but the reality is that they all won't. Unfortunately, it seems like our black youth failing is by design. Our kids face obstruction at every walk of life. They face financial hindrances, educational prohibitions, and security problems just to name a few. Black kids live in a world where they constantly have to decide what's right and what's wrong. The sad thing is that the answer to what is right and wrong could change from day to day or even minute to minute. Yes, our kids know right from wrong, but when life's circumstances constantly challenge what they know, they are going to make the wrong decision from time to time. If a kid hasn't eaten in a day, what's right and wrong is no longer of concern.

Black people are not savages or animals. We are merely people who are cast in adverse situations and are forced to deal with them. Even though we're treated as second class citizens, we're a group of people who are talented in all aspects of life. Poverty makes people do some things they'd never do under normal circumstances. If you look at any other race that is poverty stricken, they have the same attributes as black people who are poverty stricken, so stop the name calling.

Black people who are in the middle class or

higher don't commit crimes at a high rate. Instead, we're leaders of our communities and offer more than what we take. Don't judge black people because it's easy and makes you feel better about your privilege. If white America changed positions with black America, they'd do the exact same thing as poverty stricken people. If you look at the movie entitled, "Trading Places" starring Eddie Murphy, he touches on this very issue of how white people would behave the same way as black people when faced with the same predicaments. Now, that's a fictional movie, but its theme rings true in real life.

I'll use a real-life story to exemplify my point. There was a cop in South Carolina who had received awards for being a cop of high esteem. Sometime later, he was involved in a police shooting that was unjustified. Fortunately, the guy he shot wasn't killed, but the cop was fired and arrested because of the shooting. The cop was given bail, but months after his release for the shooting, he was caught shoplifting out of Walmart. This story brings to light that anyone who is in a situation where they don't have money to get what they need, will break the law to get it.

If the bull's-eye is ever lifted off the back of black America, we'll be able to shine more than we already do. Stop being afraid of our strengths and embrace them. Black people stay strong and don't ever stop striving for greatness. Educate yourselves and be empowered. We have to support each other and stop falling for the traps that are being set by the white man.

LOVE THIS BOOK AND WANT MORE?

VISIT RYANHODGEBOOKS.COM

MORE BOOKS BY RYAN

The Deception Series:
*Web of Deception**
*Wrath of Deception**
*Will of Deception**
*Rape by Deception***
*Woes of Deception**

Historical Science Fiction:
Reversed World Power

*Adult romance
**Suspense Thriller. Spin-off of other novels in series

www.ingramcontent.com/pod-product-compliance
Lightning Source LLC
Chambersburg PA
CBHW060107260626

47160CB00005B/1826